Honey I Promise

A Story of Love

BY RICK MINERD

Order this book online at www.trafford.com
or email orders@trafford.com

Most Trafford titles are also available at major online book retailers.

Printed in Victoria, BC, Canada.

ISBN: 978-1-4269-1760-8 (sc)
ISBN: 978-1-4269-1761-5 (dj)

Library of Congress Control Number: 2009936088

Our mission is to efficiently provide the world's finest, most comprehensive book publishing service, enabling every author to experience success. To find out how to publish your book, your way, and have it available worldwide, visit us online at www.trafford.com

Trafford rev. 12/3/2009

www.trafford.com

North America & international
toll-free: 1 888 232 4444 (USA & Canada)
phone: 250 383 6864 ♦ fax: 812 355 4082

D OMESTIC VIOLENCE IS a serious issue that touches almost everyone at some time. Perhaps a friend or relative, or maybe even closer... personal involvement. The laws designed to protect victims and punish abusers are better today than in decades past but the problem is not likely to go away, ever.

Human nature is what it is and although we may never know what triggers someone's temper or penchant for violence we do know that alcohol and drugs are often contributing factors.

As is jealous or suspicious emotions, or vindictive personalities and other forms of mental illness.

Any of these can accelerate the possibilities of one person hurting another, even someone they love.

And although various methods of counseling including opportunities to educate victims and abusers are offered, too few of either seek them out and some of those who do never do anything to change how or where they live, instead they remain in volatile situations until one or both suffers.

Often repeatedly.

Laws addressing these problems are ever evolving and in recent year's some of the changes in them have made it easier to identify exactly what constitutes domestic violence, including the signs that lead to it.

For instance, a person can now be charged with DV for just threatening to harm another; saying something like *"I will beat the Hell out of you"* if said to anyone who is related, shares the same household or if they have a child together is cause for being charged with domestic violence.

If the victim can articulate that they believe such a threat is real, especially if there is another reason to expect the likelihood of it such as a history of violence, or said during a drunken fit of rage causing immediate fears it can become two charges; (*Domestic violence, by menacing threats.*)

(Separate complaints.)

If such a statement includes verbiage such as *"I will blow your head off, kill you, cut your throat*, or *burn your house down"* even if no physical violence has taken place it becomes a charge of *domestic violence by aggravated menacing,* something far more serious.

Sadly, not enough people are aware of that and even though it is a sign that they may be in serious danger they either escalate the situation by responding in kind, or they forget it and hope nothing happens to them.

Reporting such a threat to the police is their best option here, yet some never do.

Another element that has been added to DV laws in recent years is the ability for police officers to file charges themselves even if the victim is either too scared or simply does not want the abuser to go to jail.

If the officer has clear evidence that an action of domestic violence has occurred and can identify the attacker, he or she is mandated by law in most states to file the complaints themselves, regardless of the wishes of the victim.

And in some cases both parties may end up with charges filed against them, and both can be taken to jail.

They cannot bond out before being brought before a judge, usually the following day or whenever court next reconvenes. In other words if someone is arrested on a Saturday they will not have an opportunity to get out of jail until Monday. This is an element of the law put in place to insure that hot-heads cannot return to their victim in the heat of the moment, or before the victim can arrange protection for themselves.

Although first offenses of domestic violence are generally classified as misdemeanors, the charges can and often are escalated into the felony category if serious physical harm has occurred, and instead of a brief stay in jail, a small fine or counseling, the offender can draw serious time behind bars.

Of particular importance, especially to law enforcement personnel, is that anyone convicted of DV loses the privilege to carry a firearm. Many people who were employed as peace officers and other public services have seen their careers ended as the result of a single DV conviction, as well as many non-public workers who have faced additional charges in addition to the original DV complaint because they had possession of a firearm after a previous domestic violence conviction.

The charge is called *weapons under disability*.

Having been convicted of domestic violence multiple times can affect a person's ability to get a job, sign a lease- and in some cases even dictate where they are allowed to live. In addition to all of this, DV convictions can change custody agreements, alter visitation privileges or forbid any contact with their victims altogether, and even forfeit voting rights.

Sometimes the physical and mental scars never go away, nor does the recorded history of the more serious abusers, it follows them forever.

Yet with all of these improvements in policing this issue and protecting people from each other the problem isn't going away, and even though police officers are receiving better training than ever in this area, a great deal of their working day is spent separating people from one another, locking up offenders and preparing evidence for prosecutors.

And there are still too many victims or potential victims who don't know how to get help or simply how to get away from bad situations.

From a law enforcement perspective the biggest frustration for me was trying to make offenders and victims alike understand all of the possible consequences. Because too many times the excuse for either staying in a bad situation or going back to one was *love*.

The feeling that one could not live without the other, yet too often that is exactly what happened anyway.

Some went to jail for a long time, and some even died simply trying to hold onto something that was never meant to be.

Although not all bad relationships end in horror, far too many of them do.

That is why I decided to share Lillian's story, it is one of strength and of hope based on love.

And even though her story begins decades ago, the similarities between her struggles and what victims still endure are many. The underlying difference is that victims now have alternatives for changing their circumstances that did not exist in the past.

I am hoping that anyone who sees themselves in the pages Lillian wrote understands why I decided to share it.

That someone may free them self of a place they should not be in.

Sam and Sadie Greenberg
1924

Chapter One

I T ISN'T KNOWN what that January day in 1925 was like for the newborn daughter of Sam and Sadie, whether she came into the world wanted or if she arrived as a burden to two people whose life together must have been *strained* at best.

Aside from the obvious conclusions that these two people were never meant to be married or have children there are hints of infidelity and maybe spousal abuse, as well as *possible* child neglect, stories left behind in what is a personal diary kept by Lillian.

A journal that leaves the second half of the 1920s full of mysteries.

Was she *unable* to remember her life as a toddler or was there some reason she chose not to?

Given all she was willing to talk about throughout her life, including many heart-wrenching details of things so personal, so terribly sad, and at times embarrassing, the possibility for either is there.

Most of this is not known because the little girl rarely spoke about her parents, about what kind of people they were, whether or not she remembered anything about living with them or what eventually caused her mother to be placed in various hospitals.

Nor is it fully disclosed why by the age of four or five she would begin a sad journey that would take her from one foster home to another. Living with strangers and being passed from one temporary family to the next until she was old enough to survive on her own.

And no one now living could possibly know exactly what life for this little girl was like, who would before the age of five find herself in a supporting role of helping to raise and comfort a younger brother when foster families were willing to take them in as a package; something that did not always happen.

Lillian, 1927

The mysteries of those earliest years of a life that would be betrayed repeatedly are among other secrets she may have kept to herself, secrets that she would *never* reveal before she passed away. One might wonder if Lillian took to the grave memories of something so dark or too embarrassing for her to share with anyone.

Perhaps just as perplexing is why she decided to write a diary documenting what was *good* about growing up in Cleveland Ohio during the *"Great Depression"* and how she was used by some who took her in to cook, wash dishes, do laundry, scrub toilets and floors and run errands while her foster brothers and sisters were pampered.

She could articulate in great detail, descriptions of some people she loved and who helped her and her brother through some emotional times, and of how her brother was sometimes not allowed to enter some of those homes through a door like everyone else, instead having to go in and out through a basement window.

Of watching others in her temporary families open holiday gifts while she and her brother were there seemingly only to pick up discarded wrapping paper and boxes and carry them outside. Never suggesting that she or her brother went totally without, but hinting of less than equal treatment.

Still, Lillian found herself in the company of a few who understood what she was living through. Sometimes it was a foster sibling… or more often a friend at school.

In addition, always on the sidelines like a guardian angel, her aunt Edith, Sadie's sister.

Perhaps with reasons of her own to observe from a distance and to be as close as possible if needed in an emergency.

Lillian wrote of her love for Edith not only in her diary but in greeting cards and letters throughout her entire life.

Hank and Lillian 1928

"I don't remember my first five years of life except that my brother Harry (Hank) and I lived with our grandparents until I was five and he was three. I remember that Grandpa owned a lot of property, including a four family house and a two family home. He also worked as a tailor for a great many years.

Grandma was a very sweet person but I only remember her as being sick, so Aunt Edith took care of us.

My grandparents had five children, Esther, Sadie (my mother), Sol, and Gertrude (who were twins) and of course Edith. Grandma also had a twin sister.

I guess when I was five years old we were removed from their home and placed in a foster home with the Rappaport family. They lived at 1211 East 111ᵗʰ Street in Cleveland Ohio.

The family included Sarah and Harry Rappaport, their daughter Arline and sons Sam and Willy (Bill) - Bill's wife Mary, and their niece from Hamburg Germany, Senta.

They took in other foster children as well, including Patty, Lucy, Clara and Clarissa (twins), and Marlene and Ethel. Those kids were lucky. Eventually they went back to their parents.

However Hank and I never did. Our mother was too sick to care for us, and well, our dad lived in Detroit, Michigan. Evidently, the courts did not think he was capable of caring for us.

Dad was deaf and we later learned that he was married to another woman before he married our mother. Later in life we learned that he had another son by his first wife.

His name was Manny, but we rarely saw him."

This first entry into Lillian's diary offers only a glimpse into the confusion that must have been her earliest years. However, it offers hints of what would eventually mold her into becoming one day something of an overly protective mother, and a wife who would spend several years forgiving and making excuses for the torments and abuses of a husband.

A man who was domineering, and one who often left her to struggle alone as he went about living a life of hell-raising and infidelity.

Perhaps it was a sense of needing to belong to a family, even if it was a terribly dysfunctional one.

Maybe as an adult her memories of being abandoned as a child by those who owed it to her to care more about the responsibility of raising her and her brother were among the reasons she tolerated the horrible circumstances she would eventually find herself living in.

Often left alone in strange towns sometimes hundreds of miles from the familiar surroundings of Cleveland Ohio, trying to understand the differences between the well-to-do, strict and very polished Jewish people who took turns raising her, and the family of mostly limited education, often ill mannered and *politeness challenged* that she would marry into at a young age.

Lillian's collection of memories also explains a mystery to some about a life that did not include any strong sense of religious preference.

Although born to parents of the Jewish faith and raised by Orthodox Jewish families, she rarely offered any clue of her own faith.

Never, to anyone who knew her well did she even suggest one faith preference over another, or criticize or question anyone else's beliefs. She did believe in God though, and she lived what most people who pay attention to such things might describe as a saintly life.

Churches to her were beautiful places regardless of what the person at the pulpit preached.

She did not attend one on a regular basis but she could not pass one without remarking on its beauty, or the beauty of it anytime she attended a wedding or any other ceremony that required a house of worship as a backdrop. Those who did not bother to ask would never have guessed that she did not *belong* to any particular faith.

Living in run down tenements or country shacks, sometimes out of suitcases in the homes of relatives or friends after she was coaxed out of Cleveland could not have been what Lillian hoped for when she was swept off her feet by the man she would eventually marry.

In fact, it is easy to assume that her written memories of that first foster family who took her and Hank in are an outline of what she considered the best times of her life.

Times she would miss as an adult, especially when introduced to her new in-laws, and would begin a long journey that few would ever hope to take.

Chapter Two

"*T*HE *R*APPAPORT'S *HAD* a nice home; it had eight rooms and a bath, an attic and a basement, and a nice yard with a garden, a cherry tree and two mulberry trees. The big trees in the front yard were kept whitewashed. (Lower half of the trunk was painted white, as some did in those days.)*

Harry and I attended Parkwood Elementary School.

I remember I started in afternoon kindergarten and my teacher's name was Mrs. Warren. I remember the naps we had to take. Once at the end of the school year she took us on a picnic. Everyone was nice.

Hank and I learned to adjust.

I met a girl in the neighborhood who became my best friend. Miriam and I remained close the rest of our lives, even when times and circumstances would eventually separate us by thousands of miles.

I would remain in Ohio and she would eventually marry a criminal lawyer and settle in Paradise Valley, Arizona. Her brother Ray would end up in Columbus where he became a professor and a drama coach at the Ohio State University."

It seemed important to Lillian that others knew of her past associations with people of various successes, perhaps because there were so many in her life who disappointed her or embarrassed her.

Maybe she feared some would judge her by the failures of those sometimes closet to her.

People she should have been able to place her trust and confidence in but instead made life more challenging for her.

When possible she was more than eager to sing the praises of those she cared about, and seemingly obliged to make it clear that she grew up surrounded by opportunities for a better life, some that would be out of her reach.

Not because of her ability, but for the efforts of others who wanted to control her, or isolate her from the rest of the world, claiming her as if she were a *personal* possession.

"I remember my first grade teacher, Miss Wolf. She was nice. At age seven I was in the second grade and Mrs. Mackleroy was my teacher, and when I was in the third grade, my teacher was Miss Hempy.

Those were good days.

By then I had two more very close friends, one was Margaret Mary Worthington and the other was Marie Foley. Along with Miriam the four of us would play jump rope (double dutch) and hopscotch. In the summer we would play under a water hose and play with our dolls. All of us had roller skates, and skating along the city sidewalks was fun.

That year (1933) I had my one and only birthday party. My mother sent me a wristwatch. Someone else gave me a set of little China dishes and an Orphan Annie book. It was fun.

Then when I was nine years old and in the fourth grade I was the teacher's pet. My teacher, Miss Horowitz would send me to Sugarman's grocery store to buy her lunch.

She would pay me a quarter for going.

At home I had to wash the dishes, that was my job.

I also received my first pair of eyeglasses that year.

The Rappaport's were good to Hank and I then. For good deeds we would receive change to purchase candy, or sometimes a soda from the soda fountain at a corner candy store-- owned by Mr. and Mrs. Kantor.

If you were lucky and got either a gold or a silver gumball from the machine you would win two huge candy bars.

Hank and I always shared our candy."

That same year I was taken to the movie theatre for the first time. The Rappaports took Hank and I to see a James Cagney gangster movie. That was exciting."

Lillian, Sadie and Hank
1931

Whatever life was like for Lillian and Hank before they joined the Rappaport family there could not have been too much affection or warm emotions shown to them. In her diary she mentions that she does not remember much before the age of five, but her memories throughout her elementary school years were written in vivid details.

Moreover, she expresses nothing but love for the Rappaports, stating in one paragraph, *"The Rappaports were the second love of my life."*

If so Aunt Edith must have had top billing.

Edith 1934

"Edith was our favorite aunt. She came to visit us every Saturday. She brought us candy, and gave us money for the movies.

We would go to the Liberty Theatre on Saturday afternoons where kids younger than twelve years old were admitted for a dime. There were usually two movies for the price of one (double features) and they would show a cartoon, newsreels, and upcoming attractions.

They would also show short features that were like serials. Those would continue for up to twelve weeks keeping us in suspense and wanting us to return week after week.

When I was ten years old I was in the fifth grade and my teacher was Mrs. Warmeling.

She was nice and gave she me a book called "The Dog of Flanders."

It became my most cherished possession.

At home, Mr. and Mrs. Rappaport belonged to a bridge club; there were ten couples in the group and they took turns playing cards in each other's homes from week to week. When it was our turn to host, and if Hank and I were good we were allowed to dress up and go to the movies.

On the other hand, if we were bad, and that did not take much, we were whipped with a belt.

Discipline was key then.

When I was eleven, and in the sixth grade my teacher was Miss Betty. I remember being sad most of the time that year because I knew it was my last at Parkwood Elementary.

Nevertheless, when graduation day came it was a special day. The girls wore white blouses and navy blue skirts, and the boys wore white shirts and long pants.

I would miss playing tag on the fire escapes and all of the fun we had on the playground for those six years. I guess I was sort of growing up."

Compared to the life that awaited her south of the Lake Erie shores later it would appear that Lillian made the most of her childhood years.

In spite of living with strangers at this young age instead of in a loving home with her own parents, her diary reveals a child that seems well adjusted, but also one who knew the difference between how she and Hank were treated and a few others, including the other kids who eventually went home to their families.

To her they were the *lucky* ones.

Discipline being the *key* that she wrote about was probably something expected, and perhaps accepted for the price of having what we would now think of as innocent childhood fun. Having to earn what many children now receive just because they are children, or because they expect it.

Nowhere in her diary does she indicate any behavior on her part or Hanks, or for that matter on the part of any of her friends that would warrant whippings with belts.

In today's environment that would be considered domestic violence by assault.

However as she would explain later they could be whipped for talking back to elders, or for questioning *any* form of authority, or for not keeping their rooms clean or for allowing a vulgar word to cross their lips.

As she stated in the diary *"It didn't take much.*

But in those days and even in more recent years, whipping children with belts was not that uncommon and wasn't viewed as any form of assault, for many, kids were fair game for such punishment if they got out of line.

Regardless of how some may view this form of punishment, it is an act of violence and one that can pass through generations. Adults who have faced assault charges for whipping their own kids will commonly say that is how they were disciplined as children.

One of the problems with that analogy is that some believe that violence is the answer to controlling everyone around them, including other adults, not excluding their spouse.

Discipline or another's definition of it was something also waiting for Lillian as she grew into a woman and would become the wife of a real abuser, one whose actions will become even less understood.

Experiences she would endure at the hands of the man she would marry, and sometimes at the hands of in-laws, abuses that may even make those early whippings seem like fond memories, or maybe less traumatizing.

The Rappaports, although strict by Lillian's description were people she called her *second love.*

"I remember when we got our first record player. We had a Gene Krupa record called "Drum Boogie." I loved that song and loved playing it, although we were not allowed to touch the record player.

I only did it when the Rappaport's were not home, which by the way was often.

Hank and I were home alone a lot.

Sometimes they would take us to visit their relatives where we were expected to be seen, but not heard. The whole family was strict, and if we were offered a piece of candy we thought that was really something.

At home I earned my keep by doing chores. Things like scrubbing floors on my hands and knees and washing dishes, but I was occasionally rewarded with movie fare.

I was twelve years old then.

That year I baby-sat for some friends of the Rappaport's who had two little girls and I was paid thirty cents a night. Their grandmother would make us Postum with crackers for a snack and allowed us to listen to "Our Hit Parade" on the radio.

I liked sitting there on Saturday nights because I could hear all of the latest hit songs on the radio, and because there was a sharp boy who lived next door!

He was fourteen.

On Sunday mornings I would walk home with my thirty cents, stop at the drug store, and buy Mrs. Rappaport a pack of cigarettes, (she smoked Phillip Morris) and I would use the other fifteen cents for the movies.

By then the Andy Hardy movies were my favorite but I also enjoyed Mickey Rooney, Judy Garland, Deanna Durbin, June Allyson, Abbot and Costello and anything by my all-time favorite, Shirley Temple."

"Earn her keep?" In a home where this child lived, not by choice but because it is where someone in authority decided she had to?

The innocence of youth, the willingness to *behave*, be polite and question nothing, especially when speaking to her elders, it was typical for the times.

Lillian sounds like she was a typical pre-teen in the 1930s.

Certainly not spoiled or given anything she did not deserve, but given what she wanted and needed most, a home, and hopefully a family who cared about her.

As she would grow through this era and eventually try to figure out how to make it on her own, one might think that any *smooth talker* could dazzle her and sweep her off her feet.

She would meet several who would make promises of a lasting life together; a life away from the one that may have been painfully obvious to those she knew as friends or even boyfriends.

After all, hiding one's loneliness is not always easy, and even though Lillian spoke often of having many friends she mentions being lonely... frequently.

No question that men were dominates in her young world.

Something else that was indicative of that era.

Writing about washing dishes and calling it her job, on her hands and knees scrubbing floors and baby-sitting for spending money, things many other girls probably had to do.

In addition, spending half of her baby-sitting money to buy cigarettes for her foster mother, either an act of kindness and generosity, or it was part of the deal to be allowed to do it.

Lillian never explains that.

Nevertheless, *sharing* or forfeiting half of her earnings is something else she would later become accustomed to. Sometimes, no make that many times against her will and at great physical sacrifice.

In 1937 Lillian entered Patrick Henry Junior High School.

Lillian
Second Row-Far Right

"My first homeroom teacher at PH was Miss Stacy and I was in Room 310.

She also taught art.

Other teachers that first year were Mr. Emch (math) Mr. Likens (science) Mr. Stevenson (social studies) and Miss Arbuckle (study hall.) Miss Arbuckle was also the attendance teacher, and she was very strict.

Missing school without a good excuse would get a kid twenty full detentions. Miss Alexander was our drama teacher, and I cannot remember our gym teacher's name but she was very short and very nice.

During lunch period we could sit in the auditorium and watch twenty minutes of a movie for two cents.

I had a crush on Bob Bartles, a ninth grader. He was really sharp!

Jeannie Glover was my best friend.

Jeannie was cute and was a lot of fun to be with. We were in sewing class together and I learned how to make a diurnal skirt and a bolero jacket.

Sewing was not my favorite class but I really liked English.

I could have done without math too.

Ethel Sparks was one of the foster kids who lived with us. She was fourteen years old and really built for her age. And all the boys noticed! She took me to some boy-girl parties and to Forrest Hills Swimming Pool.

Swimming pools only cost a dime then, and once when we went to Filderbeds Pool a boy threw me into the water not knowing I couldn't swim and I nearly drowned. I never went back there.

Mrs. Rappaport hired a cleaning girl that year to come in and give the house a good going over on Fridays. Mary was her name and although she was pretty, she was lazy.

She would bring her love story magazines with her, lay across the bed and read instead of working. Therefore, she was fired and Miriam was hired. She was plump and jolly and a super good worker. She would stay until 2:00 in the morning to get her work done and all she got was $3.00, her supper and carfare home.

She was a sweet girl.

Mrs. Rappaport was a stickler for an immaculate home. I know, I had my share of responsibilities to keep it that way!"

The Rappaports

At this stage of Lillian's young life we have an image of a sweet little girl putting behind her the confusion of trying to belong, doing for the most part what she was told to do and accepting her circumstances.

Perhaps struggling with her innocence while at the same time aware that she is growing into a mature young woman. Clearly, she made friends easily and seemed to have many, and because of her diary we know that she possessed certain gifts, such as caring for others and of personal survival.

The latter being an ability she would one day have to rely on.

When growing up in the familiar surroundings of 1930s Cleveland would eventually become struggles in the late 1940s in Athens Ohio.

When sometimes instead of playing grown-up with make-up she would see a grown-up staring back from mirrors with blackened eyes, swollen lips, a bloody nose and a broken heart.

When being beaten up by a man for reasons she never understood would become routine.

Moreover, when sharing her earnings changed from doing it because it was right to doing it out of fear, or having it taken from her.

And learning the tough lessons of feeling responsible for not a little brother, but eventually for children of her own, and where her best friends would become police officers. Not because she was happy to see them, or even wanted to know them, but because she needed rescued, or because they were there looking for a wanted man.

A man who she would be married to but one who didn't seem to understand what that meant, and who would never respect her as a wife.

Whether they were sheriff's deputies, city cops or military police officers, Lillian would come to know the handsome sailor who stole her heart was not only a navy man, but would someday walk away from her and join the United States Army as well.

Two acts of patriotism that would be washed away by discharges for bad behavior.

However as a thirteen-year-old girl,

"Eighth grade was fun. Jeanie was my best friend and we had cooking class together. One day we got into trouble. We had a fire drill and I asked to be excused from school but Jeannie didn't.

When her class marched out she ran from her group and met me at the streetcar stop. We went downtown to The Palace Theatre to see a Big Band concert, and later when the school and her parents and my foster parents found out we were made to stand for our disobedience.

I don't remember what our punishment was.

Another time Jeannie stole a spoon from cooking class and made a bracelet out of it for me.

For that she was suspended and her mother removed her from PH and enrolled her in Notre Dame Academy, a school across town. And although we never again attended classes together we remained friends for years.

The following year I was in the ninth grade and I made new friends.

Among them was a girl named Irene Bauer. She, myself and my other friends, Miriam, Margaret Mary, Margaret Mulroy, Margaret Appleton, Irene, Jeannie, Marie Foley and the three Savage sisters became a close group.

Margaret Appleton was a few years older and attended Collingwood High School.

One day she walked me to school (as she had to pass mine on her way to Collingwood.)

It was such a pretty day we decided the beach would be more fun than school that day.

It was May and we figured it would be fun to wade into the water so we did.

However around noon it began to rain and we were in trouble.

We could not go to school and explain what we had done, and we could not go home.

The day became chilly so we walked up onto a strangers porch and the woman who answered the door saw us standing there shivering so she invited us in. In those days people were more trusting."

Looking for a port in what Lillian regarded as a storm that day was easier than finding refuge from different kinds of storms later, storms that would become routine after meeting her future husband in 1945.

Promising her the moon but offering little to nothing as collateral if she would marry him.

Lillian would fall in love with a dream, even though her heart convinced her that she loved a man. Probably more common among women who are easily sweet-talked than we would hope it to be.

Young women who are unable to see the forest fires beyond the horizon of smoking trees.

Not knowing what lies ahead following their acceptance of marriage proposals, especially from men they hardly know. Then finding out too late that those promises of bliss, and a life in *"Shangri-La"* were hollow.

Moreover, in Lillian's case no previous memory or romantic tales of how her father courted her mother, or reasons why her mother agreed to marry a man who apparently was not the right fit for her either. Only shared accounts and vague memories of who he was, and that he too was a smooth talker.

Not surprisingly after Lillian and the young sailor married she tried to retain a relationship with her father. Perhaps because she hoped he could become the safety net he never was when she was little, or maybe simply because she loved him, or felt obligated in some way to allow him some form of making up for valuable lost time.

Nevertheless, he and her husband would quickly come to dislike one another.

Neither trusted the other, and over time Sam, (*Lillian's father*) would also be on the receiving end of his new son-in-law's meanness and deceit.

However, less than ten years before getting married and having another man take control of her life...

"My friend Irene and I used to go roller skating at the Roller Gardens on Friday nights. We would board a streetcar sometimes and go to Euclid Beach, my favorite spot in the world.

It was sad at the end of that school year because I was getting ready to graduate from junior high and I always felt that way when I knew I had to leave a school.

I had met such wonderful girls there including Margaret Ameroso, Mary Genevesee, Tony and Clara Yaferno, Laverne Faranaci, Sammy Giagusso, another girl named Frances who we called "Bird Legs" and a few boys who were always nice, Johnny, Leone, Ray and Tommy.

As the school year was winding down we would all go to the Ambassador Theatre to watch movies together on Sunday afternoons. We knew the ushers there, two brothers named Eddie and Freddie Weishapple. Then after the movies we would sit in a soda shop next to the theatre, drink sodas and enjoy just being with each other.

We only knew the owners of the shop as "Mom" and "Pop."

That is where I got my first job, working behind the counter that year."

Working behind the counter at the soda fountain would become something of a dress rehearsal for Lillian's future. A job taken then for extra money would be training for what she would one day have to do to feed, shelter and support a husband's drinking habit and pay for his mistakes.

In addition, she would learn that she needed to support not only him and her, but eventually the couple's children, who like her would go through their earliest years and even through life itself barely knowing *their* father.

Finding low paying jobs and scrambling for baby sitters and money to pay them, with little more reward than hiding from bill collectors, getting knocked around and having to hide her earnings from an abusive drunk would sometimes become Lillian's daily routine.

And when she would discover that her tucked away money had been found and used to purchase alcohol and dazzle other women, she would not only see her utilities shut off and cry over eviction notices, she would find herself turning to friends, co-workers and far-away relatives for money to feed her children.

Sometimes getting only enough for them, while going hungry herself.

She missed the carefree days at Patrick Henry Junior High, and would reflect often on her friends and others she could trust. Reminiscing through old letters and photographs, she would write in her diary of the days when she really did not need to worry about being in trouble but did.

Trouble then no longer seemed like trouble.

Instead, those memories of being disciplined as a child may have even seemed deserved, or by the politeness she expresses in her journal, maybe fond reflections.

Memories of boys she had a crush on as a child probably caused tears to well in her eyes, maybe wondering, *"What if…?"*

"While I was working behind the counter at Mom and Pop's soda fountain I met Ernie Messaro. He had his own bike and he used to take me riding (double) on it. Sometimes he would ride me to Rockefeller Park where he would rent a rowboat and we would go boating around the lake, drifting peacefully among the many swans.

Then it came time to say goodbye to Patrick Henry Junior High.

For graduation I had to borrow a blue dress from Jeanie's sister Pat. I had my own white shoes but not a dress nice enough to wear to the ceremony.

After graduation some of us said goodbye forever but a few of us would continue to know one another for years to come.

That same year I met Chuck Regal. He was a doll! He worked at Thomkins Ice Cream Store and was always eager to give me free ice cream.

In the fall I enrolled in John Hay Senior High where the student body consisted of about 2000 girls and only five hundred boys. Across the street from John Hay was Cathedral Latin High School, an all boy's Catholic school, so the neighborhood evened itself out among the sexes."

How many times as a young adult did Lillian reflect on what sounds like past summer flings or simple crushes?

Later, after we get a look at her life as a young woman we would have to think she needed those mental revisions often.

As her married life unfolded she would find herself increasingly wondering how she landed in the spot she was in. Life in a foster home probably had its moments of sadness, and maybe even similar mental flashbacks of living with her grandparents as a very little girl.

However, life as a wife and a mother in a time and place where there were few safe havens to escape to or not enough laws to protect victims of abuse had to be traumatizing.

Living in *homes* that she would later in life refer to as *fire traps* or *bug motels*, not to mention routine mental and physical abuses, and what may have amounted to rape in place of love making, surely had to be terrifying.

Yet many times she had to wake up and anticipate that the new day would not be too different from the previous one, and that she would somehow have to figure a way out of her nightmare, as well as a way to place herself and her kids in an environment where they would not grow up with any similarities between them and the people they sometimes feared, and rarely understood.

Lillian needed a life, she certainly placed a costly down payment on one.

"I don't remember much about high school and I really don't know why. I loved school but maybe because my life was about to change and I sensed not for the better. I have chosen not to wander back to that time in my mind, or in this journal.

It was not all bad though.

I remember a teacher named Miss Wolfe who taught personal hygiene. My favorite class was typing and I remember having to buy a student pass for the streetcar to school. They were sold in the cafeteria for a quarter and were good for the week.

On nice days my friend Irene and I would walk the few miles to school through Wade Park.

That year our caseworker who handled our foster care split Hank and I up. I don't really know why, but we were sent to new foster homes. Mine was with Mr. and Mrs. Asnien who had two small daughters of their own and I became their housekeeper and baby sitter.

I was given every other Wednesday evening, and every other Saturday evening off and that allowed me time to meet with my friends where I could spend the $2.50 a week I earned working for them to earn my keep.

Compared to the Rappaport's home this one...well this one made me really miss my former foster parents.

While living with the Asniens I met a sharp guy named David O'Connor who worked for Western Union. But boy did he get me in trouble.

One Saturday night while babysitting I invited a few kids over, and when they left David had put something in the candy dish on the piano. I was not aware of what he had done but the Asnien's acted funny the next day.

That Monday when I went to school I was summoned from the study hall and told to go to the office where my caseworker was waiting for me. She had paperwork that permitted me to be taken to the juvenile detention home."

Lillian did not say in her diary what that *something* was that David had placed in the candy dish. Instead, she wrote...

"I guess they thought David and I had indulged. They kept me in the detention home for two weeks until they could find another foster family to take me in.

It was with a family named Duchon, and they had a daughter named Rowena and a son named Ronny.

They were nice people but I had to quit school to work for them to earn my room and board. I was paid $3.50 each week. That first week I bought myself a pair of skates.

My friends and I liked to go to roller rinks where we could dance and skate to the Big Band music of the day. We also went to Euclid Beach, sometimes to a movie and to the Trianson Bowling Alley, and oh yes, Dan's Gas Station.

The owner, Danny, was a heavyset jolly man who had two good-looking sons, Bob and Dick.

While living with the Duchon's I made a new friend, Helen Mahon and she quickly made friends with all of my other ones.

*While living in that foster home my father came from Detroit to
visit me.*

*He took me on a shopping spree, buying me shoes, hosiery, a
purse, a dress, slacks, a bathing suit, a birth stone ring and a skating
pin. Dad liked buying my brother and me things when he was in
Cleveland.*

*When he left he promised to return soon but it would be several
months before I would see him again."*

Trinkets of love, offered by a man she never really knew, at least
not as a father, but obviously one she respected and one might even
conclude that she may have believed that one day he would bring
her home and actually treat her like a real daughter.

Still in Lillian's journal there is no clear reasons stated why, that by
now at age sixteen she and Hank, age fourteen, were being shuffled
from one foster home to another. Why a father on the other side of
Lake Erie; living in Michigan, and who seemed to have the funds
to travel back and forth and bring presents, did not have plans in
motion to bring his children home.

Details that would never be shared.

*"Shortly after that visit I met Bob Stewart. Bob was twenty-five
years old and was attending bus driver school. He was hoping to get
a job with the Greyhound Bus Company.*

Bob was from Virginia and owned a motorcycle.

*He asked me to marry him and go back to Richmond with him and
I told him I would, but that I would first have to figure a way to run
away from home. He took my prized possessions, my roller skates (as
collateral) and told me to go home and pack.*

*I packed my suitcase (especially the new clothes my father had
bought for me) and went to stay with some friends.*

Bob still had another week of school left.

*The following Sunday I was sitting in a movie theatre with a
few girlfriends when the juvenile authorities came in, took me into
custody, and charged me with running away from home.*

*I was again placed in the juvenile detention facility and I was
heartbroken.*

*The detention home was a very lonely place, and they were
so strict. Yet I managed to make a few friends there, both named*

Dorothy. One was sent to a Catholic Convent for running away from home and the other girl and I were sent to the Blossom Hill School for girls in Brecksville Ohio.

It was pretty out there.

Dr. Warner, a lady, was the superintendent and Miss Bolik was a teacher there. Mr. and Mrs. Reynolds were the maintenance staff.

There were four cottages on the grounds as well as a main building, and I lived in one of the cottages with fourteen other girls, and we had three of the sweetest housemothers. Miss Sevela, Mrs. Heady (our cooking teacher who I came to really love, and our music teacher, a piano player named Miss Charms.

I was enrolled in waitress training and cooking, and I was in the church choir.

I remember Mayor Lauche, (who would later become the governor of Ohio) came to the school for one of our programs. I was there from August, 1941 until December, 1942. I remember hearing the news about Pearl Harbor while I was there.

Then one day I received the wonderful news that I would be going back to live with the Rappaports! By then they had moved to 10601 Hamden Avenue.

To celebrate, my grandfather gave me $50.00 to buy new clothes, so I went on another shopping spree."

Lillian was less than a year away from becoming an adult.

Going back to live with the Rappaport family was all she wanted since she was taken from their home so it must have felt like going back to the closet thing she ever knew as a family.

However, adulthood was mere months away and soon she would no longer be a ward of the courts. So does she stay with the Rappaports past her 18th birthday or is she presented with new challenges?

"When I turned eighteen I got a job at Taylor's Department Store.

My first job there was working in the hobby shop selling model car kits, model airplanes and toy trains. I later transferred to the corset department where I had to wear dark clothes, heels hose and present myself in a sophisticated manner.

I was earning $18.50 a week. Of that, I had to pay the Rappaport's $10.00 a week for room and board.

I remember going home from work and lying in bed listening to the foghorn from the D and C, (Detroit and Cleveland ship) it blew every night around 11:30 as it was leaving the dock. I bought a ticket on that ship once and took a trip to Detroit to see dad.

That was exciting…traveling alone.

Also that year I became engaged to Tommy, he had spent $350.00 on an engagement ring, which was an astronomical amount of money in those days.

I could hardly believe it!

I was so excited and proud that I talked him into taking me to Blossom Hill to visit everyone I knew there and to show off the ring. We went on Easter Sunday and it was raining very hard.

On the way back we were involved in an accident and somehow I lost the ring.

I was heartbroken, and Tommy was so furious that he broke up with me.

I had several jobs before I was twenty years old, including one at the Rola Company where I assembled radios. There I met Johnny Beck.

Another engagement, one that lasted three whole months.

Then I went to work for a company called Bishop and Babcock, they manufactured hardware for the Navy. I didn't care for it, but at least it was a job, and I needed the money to continue paying my way at home.

Then I went to work for Western Electric repairing telephones.

I liked that job, especially when I saw my first paycheck, $35.00 a week! I also worked for Warner Brothers splicing movie film they produced.

It probably sounds like I drifted from one job to another in those days and the truth is I did! Anytime I would hear of openings that paid more money, or had better benefits or better working conditions I did my best to move on.

And that happened several times.

I worked at a company called E.W. Machine where I ran a drill press all day and went home smelling like machine oil every night, then I went to work in a warehouse where I met Bob Little.

He was a very sweet guy who had long hair, wore boots, a cowboy hat, and drove an old car."

Things were looking up for Lillian as she again found herself *in love*, Bob Little appeared to be the right guy for her. They became engaged and were planning to get married.

His parents lived in the country and immediately took a liking to Lillian, and she writes in her diary that she liked them and spoke of receiving yet another engagement ring, but one that she had to return when the Rappaport's stepped in and refused to *allow* her to accept it.

Bob actually sounds like a good guy from Lillian's descriptions of him. When she tried to return the ring he was heartbroken and did not want it back. But feeling guilty, she refused to keep it and eventually persuaded him to accept it.

Strange, this time it was a guy's turn for a broken heart. Even stranger, why did the Rappaport's step in to block something that may have made her happy?

The diary does not address that issue.

As one trying to make sense of Lillian's journal and why she wrote it, I am reminded of a song written by Chris Gantry and made famous by Glen Campbell...

"She looks in the mirror and stares at the wrinkles that weren't there yesterday; she thinks of the young man that she almost married, what would he think if he saw her this way?

She picks up her apron in little girl fashion when something comes into her mind... Slowly starts dancing, remembering her girlhood and all of the boys she had waiting in line..

The photograph album she takes from the closet and slowly turns the page...And carefully picks up the crumbling flower...The first one he gave her now withered today.

She closes her eyes, and touches the housedress that suddenly disappears...And just for a moment she's wearing the gown that broke all their minds back so many years....

****The song "Dreams of the Everyday Housewife" by Chris Gantry.*

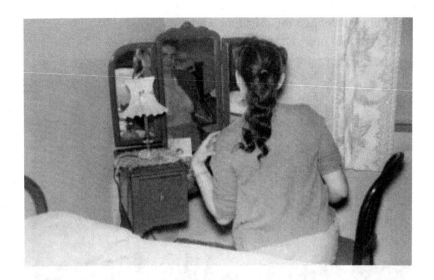

It would seem Lillian was offered marriage proposals as frequently as she was jobs.

Meet Larry Warren.

"Larry and I met after my relationship with Bob ended.

I swear he was a dead ringer for one of my favorite movie stars, Clark Gable. He and I became very close and one day he showed up with an engagement ring.

Here we go again.

Along with a pendant watch and even a wristwatch that he had talked his mother into giving me.

I loved him, I really loved him.

His mom was also very nice and she worked hard at a laundry, and he had a brother who was also very nice but his father was rather mean. But the more Larry and I spent time with each other the more possessive and jealous he became. I could not look at another man, or even answer one if I was spoken to.

Soon we were fighting over that a lot. So...."
They broke up.

Lillian in Cleveland
1943

Chapter Three

L ILLIAN MOVED AWAY from home in 1945 when Mr. Rappaport passed away.

Mrs. Rappaport was ill herself and after selling the home she moved in with other relatives, leaving Lillian with no choice but to move. Finally on her own, in a rented room with no one to make up rules for living under *their roof…* this was hers to come and go as she pleased.

But soon after getting her own place…

"I got sick in April, 1945 and had to spend two weeks in a hospital.

When I was well I rented a sleeping room from two old ladies, Mrs. Strack and Miss Mack. I had also gotten a job at the Carter Hotel as a waitress at the luncheonette counter.

That's where I met…"

Another man with a marriage proposal?

Maybe he will be *"the one."*

But before we meet him let's consider her life up till now.

Growing up in foster homes with very strict foster parents who would sometimes whip her with a belt, and where she had to work to *"earn her keep"* and living sometimes in detention facilities, during the Great Depression, and she has seen the start of a world war.

She has shared very little about her real mother and speaks of rare visits by her father-who when she does reference him she speaks glowingly despite his obvious absence *and* of the many come and go proposals of marriage, yet still another opportunity awaits.

And in spite of the many disappointments of wanting to be loved, to find a real home that would truly be hers and be surrounded by a family, only to face one let down after another, she still sounds upbeat.

Working now at the Carter Hotel, an upscale hostelry built just fifteen years earlier in downtown Cleveland near the Union Train Depot, she was in a pretty good spot to meet all sorts of travelers.

Maybe even that so-called *right guy.*

After all, here was a pretty, young woman with what is clearly a friendly and sweet disposition who has shown a history of being on the receiving end of much attention by the guys she met.

Hell, they all wanted to marry her!

A diamond in the rough, in a tough city during tough times, and at a disadvantage in some ways, brought on by her naivety and an undaunted willingness to trust others, especially those who approach with seemingly good intentions and sometimes false promises.

In short, she was a sitting duck for those whose intentions might not have been what they presented.

People we now think of as predators.

Guys like…

" Bucky…I had been working at the Carter Hotel for a few weeks, when one night my girlfriend Josephine and I were walking through Coney Island on Ninth Street and he and a Coast Guard buddy, (Bucky was a sailor) approached us and we became acquainted.

He was so handsome in his uniform and what a gift of sweet talk! He told me that he had just returned from overseas and was on a thirty-day furlough heading home to see his folks in Athens Ohio.

For whatever reason his train had stopped in Cleveland and he decided to stay for a few days.

Working at the hotel every day from 5:00 PM until 1:00 AM I would find him hanging around late at night waiting for me to finish.

He would order food and play songs on the jukebox, and he would pester me to go walking with him after my shift. A few times he and I would walk down to Willard Park by the lake and talk for hours, and within a few days he was asking me to marry him.

Here we go again!

Bucky and Lillian
1945

When he finally got around to boarding a bus to Athens he asked me to promise that I would follow him the next week, and to make plans to get married. I do not have the words to explain why I did, except that even with the many friends I knew, I was still very lonesome.

When I told my friend Gus at Coney Island what I had planned to do he warned me about giving up my freedom for a guy I hardly knew, then he handed me ten dollars, bought me a soda and wished me well.

I guess I believed that by marrying Bucky I would finally be able to have a real family, and a real home of my own.

The following Saturday I bought a bus ticket and headed for Athens.

When I arrived, Bucky and his little brother, Hobart (Hobie) who was only four years old met me at the bus station. They were dressed in matching sailor uniforms, and looked very cute together.

I was experiencing something so new and so exciting, traveling alone to an area where I actually might be getting married, (for real) and on the verge of meeting my new family, wondering what they would think of me, and if they would accept me.

In those days Athens did not have city busses or taxi cabs, or if they did Bucky claimed they didn't, so we hitch-hiked and finally got a ride to his mother's house.

It seemed his whole family was there.

His mother and father, brother's Chad, Dick, and Hobie, his sister's Sara, Lovie and Deanna. Plus, there were a few aunts and uncles and a few cousins there, as well as several friends.

Another brother, Evan was away on duty with the army. (Two more brothers, Raymond and Guy had not been born yet.)

That day we all took off our shoes, sat on the grass, ate watermelon and just spent time trying to get to know one another. I really enjoyed meeting his folks.

It was fun that day.

That same night he convinced his Uncle Val to drive us to Gallipolis, Ohio to get married. Val had a blue convertible and naturally Bucky's mother wanted to tag along. I sensed she wasn't too sure I was the right girl for her son.

When we arrived we learned that we could not get married until Monday, so we decided to stay down there until we could get a blood test, get our license, and find a Justice of the Peace to marry us, instead of driving all the way back to Athens and then back to Gallipolis again."

This first weekend with her new in-laws might have been an omen for Lillian that she would have been better off to have stayed in Cleveland and waited a little longer for a shot at finding that home with a loving family to share it with.

Stating that "*Naturally Bucky's mother wanted to tag along*" would suggest there would be issues with her.

In fact, Lillian would later recount having many issues with her new mother-in-law, most of them over whether or not Buck's abuse and neglect was justified, and sometimes about how much money Lillian was able to bring to "their" table.

She would also experience other issues and challenges with a few of the brothers, as well as a few others in the family.

"I learned quickly that Bucky was not only attracted to me, but to nearly every pretty girl who came within a few feet of him, and some who were doing their best not to. He was not only a blatant skirt chaser; he was AWOL from the Navy.

However, he didn't seem worried about that.

Or even worried that I knew of his appetite for other girls.

We had our first significant quarrel a few days after we were married when he wanted me to travel somewhere out in the country to visit some of his other relatives. I was sick and did not feel like traveling, so he and his mother went without me.

Being in strange surroundings and with people who were still unfamiliar to me, I was hurt that he would leave me alone with them. But later that evening I started feeling guilty, thinking I was wrong to expect him to put my feelings before his, so I convinced Val to take me out there.

When we arrived, I was hoping he would be glad to see me, but he wasn't there.

And when Val told me that, I only wanted to go back to Athens, but he told me to wait in the car and that we would go back soon. I wound up waiting until his wife washed her hair, and his grandmother made homemade ice cream for him.

When we finally got back home his mother told me that he and his brother were downtown with the girls who lived next door.

That night I stayed outside, sitting on a swing in the yard, wondering, what did I get myself into?

When he finally got home around 2:00AM, he was making jokes and pretending that he couldn't understand why I was upset, claiming that he only went to visit a few friends. But when it became clear to him that I didn't believe him and that I felt lied to and betrayed, he promised he would never again do anything ever again to hurt me.

We spent the next few hours arguing, he even accused me of starting the whole thing and before it was over he had me feeling guilty for having gotten mad in the first place.

Cleveland seemed like a thousand miles away."

It may as well have been a million.

Lillian would find herself in similar and many times worse situations of depression and betrayal over the next ten-plus years. Situations that would also leave her stranded with *no* means to travel the miles she would need to go.

Of the brothers she had already met, only Dick showed any sympathy toward her for the wrongs she was yet to experience. Dick or, *Dickie* as she called him was also a soldier in the United States Army.

It would be discovered later that he had a heart disease and would die very young.

Young Hobart, the four-year-old brother who along with Bucky met her at the bus depot when she first arrived in Athens would also die young several years later, shot by Georgia State Troopers moments after robbing a bank in Atlanta.

And one of the brothers not yet born, Raymond would die one day after accidentally setting himself on fire.

Lillian was clearly out of her element in Southern Ohio, this was certainly not the Rappaport family, or for that matter any of the other polished people she lived with back up north.

"While during my first stay in Athens, Bucky was picked up by the military police and sent back to camp in Great Lakes Illinois, so I decided to go back to Cleveland where I got my old room back at Mrs. Strack's, and again went to work for the Carter Hotel.

I did not want to be stuck in Athens with those people.

About two weeks later he called me from New York, (collect) and said that his only punishment for being AWOL was to be assigned extra duty and that he had been transferred to a new base. He said that if I would send him some money he could come home on a weekend pass, and that he also needed money for cigarettes.

So I wired him the money and he did come home.

He arrived in Cleveland to pick me up and again we traveled to Athens to see his folks. I wasn't real excited about going back there but he assured me that things would be better.

But on the way down there he confided that he had met and spent some time with a call girl named Anne at the Waldorf Astoria Hotel in New York, but he said she meant nothing to him.

Shortly after arriving in Athens he decided to go AWOL again.

So we returned to Cleveland and he asked me to give up my room, so I did and we rented a "housekeeping apartment." that had two rooms. It was rather shabby but it was all I could afford.

Bucky had talked his mother and father into coming to Cleveland, and they got an apartment next to ours. I got a new job at Mel's truck stop and talked the owner into also hiring Bucky. I was a waitress and he was a cook. We even helped his dad find a job at a whiskey warehouse.

One day while I was working and Bucky had the day off he took his mother shopping and bought her a necklace and a bracelet. Actually, he purchased it on a time payment plan and forged my signature as a cosigner.

(I didn't know that at the time.)

I thought this was odd because he never bought me anything, not even a wedding ring.

His mother and father didn't like Cleveland so they moved back to Athens.

Bucky wanted me to quit my job and go back down there with him and I refused. He told me if I wanted to stay married to him I would have to go with him because he wanted to move in with his folks and didn't want to be alone.

I still refused so he left without me."

I guess some people take their wedding vows literally and do the best they can to honor them, through sickness and health, for better or worse and for richer or poorer, but we on the sidelines of other people's troubles have to wonder sometimes, *Why!*

Those closest to victims of bad reunions are expected to advise their friend, or a loved one to know when they have made a mistake, when to move on and put those troubles behind them.

Forsaking all others, so help you God?

Regardless of what your spouse puts you through, even if it is abundantly clear that you have been duped instead of loved.

Many do that, some until it is too late.

But maybe Bucky did love Lillian, who he always called Anne. That must have been a name he liked, it wasn't hers, as a matter of fact her middle name was Elizabeth and she preferred to be called "Lizzie."

Maybe when he looked for a hooker in New York he specifically found one named Anne only because he missed her and was home-sick. Perhaps that is what he meant when he told her the other Anne meant nothing to him.

Right.

Maybe he made up the tale about a hooker named Anne to test the waters for future adventures, or maybe he called all of his women by that name.

I'm guessing that story was more about scaring Lillian, and reminding her that there were other women out there even if he had to pay them, who could easily replace her if she didn't walk his chalked lines or didn't buckle to his demands or allow him certain freedoms.

Saying that the other woman's name was also Anne sounds a bit suspicious.

For whatever reason Lillian chose to stay around, she was at least honoring her side of the promises made when two people marry, although few probably understood why.

Most of her friends and other people who **did** care about her probably would have gotten it if she had simply walked away from a bad situation and left her husband to be dealt with by the military who was again looking for him.

It absolutely has to be concluded that she did love him. His feelings toward her might suggest that he cared very little, if at all about her, but such conclusions cannot be that easily drawn.

The fact is he did love her.

Certainly not in the way she wanted him to, or in any imaginable normal way. But this man was a weakling, clearly dependant on others for *everything*. His parents to provide food and shelter, the navy to spank him when he was bad, other people to transport him from place to place, and now a wife to bail him out of his many self-imposed problems.

He loved her, if for no other reason than because she had a weak constitution, and because it was easy to take advantage of her and take from her whatever he needed.

"While Bucky was still back in Athens living with his folks a girl named Mary moved into the apartment next to mine.

She was very nice and we became very good friends. I made the mistake of writing to him and mentioning her and right away he wrote back making vulgar comments, fearing that Mary and I were running around with other men.

(He was insanely jealous.)

So he hitched a ride back to Cleveland, still AWOL from the navy and showed up asking for money. I was still working for Mel so I borrowed $20.00 against my pay and gave it to him.

But before he could spend it that night, the Shore Patrol showed up and knocked on the door and when he looked out and saw them he ran upstairs and hid in the attic. They went up after him, brought him down and took him away.

He was sent back to Great Lakes where he spent the next six months in the Brig.

(Military jail.)

A few days later his mother showed up in Cleveland and came to Mel's where she sat at a table waiting for me to get off work. Mel was getting agitated because she wasn't buying anything and we had paying customers waiting to be seated.

I was so embarrassed.

When my shift was finally over she told me that since Bucky could not keep up the payments on the jewelry he had bought for her on a time plan, that I would be responsible for the debt. She reminded me that he had forged my name on the loan as a cosigner and that if I didn't pay for it they would be after me.

The bill had been $5.00 a week and $20.00 was still owed, so I gave her the money, plus bus fare so she could go back to Athens.

She didn't even say thank you.

Shortly after that I left Mel's and went to work at the Miller Drug Store in the Cleveland Hotel. I was once again working at the luncheonette counter and I worked with some very nice people, but Mr. Shapiro was the boss and he was a flirt.

While I was working there, Bucky's brother, Evan had learned of my whereabouts and started showing up at my job. He was on furlough from the army, and although he had brought his girlfriend with him, several times he would make passes at me and give me a rough time when I refused him. It didn't seem to matter to him that I was married to his brother, and his girlfriend seemed too timid or too scared to object to his behavior.

Although Buck was temporarily tucked away in a military brig, and most of her in-law problems were nearly 210 miles south of Cleveland the side effects of marrying into a family so seemingly dysfunctional and completely different from any she had ever known previously would change her forever.

She would have to learn new survival skills.

Evan was an intimidating man, a guy who Lillian often described as something of a bully and he was becoming yet another thorn in her life. Hitting on her the first time he met her and in the presence of his girlfriend, and more in-laws yet to be met. Some of them vying for her attention and jockeying for position to replace Bucky if he didn't want her, or for a spot in line to get dibs on any money she might come home with.

Which was something else that made her attractive to a few of them, she always seemed to have a job or friends she might be able to lean on for emergency assistance, even if only for a few dollars here and there.

A pretty girl barely out from under foster care where she had been raised in very strict and controlled environments, hoping to make it on her own with no biological mother or father close by to watch over her, and desperately seeking *some way* to distance herself from her cooped up past.

Surely Buck had shared this information about her with his family.

A dream girl, especially to anyone with predatory intentions.

Those 210 miles that separated Cuyahoga County from Athens County did not seem that far, for some Cleveland was just up the road. Moreover, a few of them would find their way to her doorstep on more occasions than they were welcome.

Meanwhile Bucky was in the brig, writing poetic love letters to his bride.

Dearest Darling Anne,

Whatever moon may meet the dawn, or stars look down on me, I promise you that I will spend the hours and the years to bring you every happiness and keep away your tears.

To cherish and to honor you with loyalty and pride and never doubt your loving lips or ever leave your side.

Whatever sun may light the sky…or fortune come along, I promise you that every day will be a brighter song… I promise you with all my heart that I will live for you and I will never rest until all of your dreams come true.

Your loving husband,
Junior

He would write such poetry often and she would keep them all stuffed in a shoebox where she would save them and take them out one by one and read them through the years, eventually those pieces of paper with poetic expressions of promises and love would number more than one hundred.

Words of love and of promises to be a better man when he got home, a man she would be proud of and the *one* who would help her realize all of her dreams, to spend her life in a loving home, with a loving family.

(*Junior* was Buck's nick-name, he was named after his father)

"Bucky had written to me asking that I come and visit him in the brig. His letters always contained pretty poetry and always sounded heartfelt. They gave me comfort and hope anytime I was feeling lonely. So on the weekends I would take a train to Chicago and from there another one to Great Lakes. I made the mistake of telling him about his brother Evan and he became furious.

He tried to imply that it was somehow my fault, that perhaps I led him on.

After assuring him that I did not, he talked of going after his brother, but I was able to persuade him to let it drop. I knew I should have just left it alone and tried to work that problem out by myself.

On one of those trips to see him I met a girl named Rose, (Dotie) and we became pen pals for life.

The trips to visit him were expensive, and very tiring but I did not mind, I felt bad for him and for what he had gotten himself into, and I wanted him to know that I did love him, and that I would be waiting for him when he came home.

Five months later he was given a bad conduct discharge from the navy and returned to Cleveland where I was still working in the drugstore. He would come in and flirt with the girls I worked with and we would quarrel about his arrogance, I would tell him how embarrassing it was for me but he always laughed and swore he was just being friendly.

On the night of my twenty- first birthday he promised to take me to see the movie "Centennial Summer" after I finished work. When my shift was over and he failed to show up to pick me up I walked across the street and found him sitting in the London Grill with two girls I worked with.

When I asked him if we were still going to the movies he became belligerent and started showing off for the girls, making fun of me and taunting me.

He was drunk.

Embarrassed, and hurt, I walked out and went to the movies myself. It was a late show, and when I got home he was waiting for me, still drunk and madder than H-E-L-L. So mad that he began screaming at me and beating me.

Funny, every time he would beat me up he would later apologize and ask if I was still his "baby doll" and he would promise to never

*raise another hand to me. Even though I didn't believe him, I believed
that he could change.*

I prayed he would change."

Lillian's diary surfaced after she passed away, nearly forty years
after her marriage to Bucky was over. And although a few very close
family members knew the marriage was rocky and often abusive,
many of the details written in her diary were not known. But the
fact that she was writing it suggests to me that she wanted someone,
if only her family to understand where she had come from, what her
life was truly like and why that marriage failed after less than fifteen
years.

That marriage actually failed after less than fifteen days, it only
went on for years.

In an era where old photographs, and in the movies that were
made then, we often view scenes depicting people nicely dressed,
living in pretty homes, men driving nice cars, opening doors for
women, and celebrating life in polite societies.

We see a backdrop of big, beautiful cars moving about in the
glow of neon lights and we sometimes think of the 1940s, especially
the second half of that decade as an exciting and romantic era; as
Lillian described her life as a teenager.

Hanging out with her neighborhood chums and going to theatres,
skating rinks and soda fountains, taking strolls on the beaches of
Lake Erie and dating guys with convertibles and motorcycles.

It was a dress rehearsal for the 1950s, still a few years away but
looming.

However, the late '40s for Lillian was something entirely different,
only a decade earlier she was a happy teenager surrounded by friends
and having fun, being taken for rides on bicycles and motorcycles,
skating and dancing and never imagining what lied ahead.

Rusted automobiles and pick-up trucks, some of them probably
held together with nails and bailing wire, traveling down country
roads and no one opening car doors for her, no pretty homes, no
fancy clothes to dress up in and certainly not surrounded by a polite
society.

Especially at home.

But before getting married she and her girl friends were just
regular *"Bobby Soxers,"* a moniker derived from the era when

white cotton stockings were worn under saddle shoes and city girl's musical tastes were for the Big Bands of Goodman and Dorsey and crooners like Frank Sinatra.

But Bucky was determined to transform his *"baby doll"* into a country girl, one that he would eventually keep barefooted and pregnant. He wanted one more at home around Ernest Tubb and Hank Williams records.

One who would serve him, maybe open *his* doors and be completely out of her comfort zone, away from living in a big city and away from being among friends. He wanted a girl that would have to live under the watchful eye of his mother, where tabs on her could be kept during all of his intended absences away from her, and where she would not have the convenience of hailing a cab, or hopping a bus to get away if she needed to.

It would seem that in his mind that she was his property, like a toy, maybe a *baby doll* that he could play with when he wanted to and shove aside when he was finished. That's what he meant when he asked her after pounding on her if she was still his.

"In 1946 my dad bought a small house in Detroit and he opened a tailoring business.

He invited us to move there, live in the home and help run his business but Bucky didn't want to, instead he decided we should move back to Athens and go back to living with his folks. I wanted to take dad up on his offer but Bucky threatened to leave me for good if I didn't go with him.

So we headed south and lived for a while with his parents. (Again.)

They had moved far out into the country to Sugar Creek Ohio near Athens, and into a dumpy little house that had no indoor plumbing and I managed to get a job at Blackmore's Restaurant as a waitress. I had to ride a Greyhound Bus back and forth to work. The restaurant was near the Ohio University campus and most of our customers were college kids so I didn't receive much in the way of tips.

One night while arguing over my meager earnings his mother tried to hit me with a chair but Bucky stopped her. Apparently I wasn't bringing home enough money for them, even he thought I was holding money back and not being truthful about what I made each day.

After that incident we decided to come to Columbus where we stayed for a while with his cousins, Betty and Blaine, they lived on East Mound Street and South High Street and I found a job as a waitress at George's Coney Island on West Broad Street.

I had an opportunity for a better paying job at David Davies Meat Packing Company but Bucky wouldn't allow me to take it. He thought the guy's working there would be too fresh, that they would flirt with me. And even though it would have given us more money and offered better benefits I still wasn't permitted to take it.

A few weeks later we headed back to Cleveland and found a housekeeping room at Mrs. Wars Rooming House. I soon found a job at Green's Drug Store working behind the luncheonette counter from 4:30 PM until 1:00 AM. I really liked that job because I had two great bosses there, Mr. Green and Mr. Levy, and I worked with a great bunch of girls, (Edna, Frankie, Grace, Eleanor, Margie and Willa.)

Many of our customers were guys from Warner and Swasy, (a factory across the street from the store.) Bucky knew that and he would constantly ask if any of them ever tried to be nice to me, or just talk to me. He always seemed to worry.

While I worked, he hung out in several beer joints on the west side where he would drink too much and then come home in a bad mood, it seemed all of his problems were somehow my fault.

One night when I came home from work he was drunk, and when he saw me he jumped up and punched me in the face, then he punched me in the stomach and knocked the wind out of me. He was mad about something but really didn't say about what. When I would ask what he was upset about he would just get worse.

Another night, New Years Eve, 1947, I walked into Shay's Bar and saw him making love to a barmaid on a table. He ordered me to leave so I went home feeling very lonely. I sat up crying until he got home, and when he walked in he handed me a wilted flower and said his girlfriend didn't want it. That too was my fault I guess.

A wilted flower?

A sad parallel to the twenty-two year old wife who he had written to from a military jail cell just months before saying,

"I promise every day will be a brighter song, I promise you with all my heart that I will live for you, and never rest until all of your dreams come true.."

Every day a brighter song, and never rest until all of your dreams come true?"

Actually, it was the same old song and maybe he knew that her dreams were really nightmares, those he could make come true.

It's no surprise that old Buckaroo wasn't doing too well as a civilian.

Rarely does Lillian mention any jobs he may have had, whereas *she* seemed capable of finding work wherever they moved to. But away from the regimentation of the navy he doesn't sound like he was a guy who was likely to settle down or maybe find work, and contribute much more than pain and suffering to a marriage that had been doomed from the day they exchanged nuptials.

So what could he possibly do to show Lillian that he meant it when he wrote in that poem…

"I promise you that I will spend the hours and the years, to bring you every happiness and keep away your tears, to cherish and to honor you with loyalty and pride, and never doubt your loving lips or ever leave your side?"

She explained it this way….

"He decided to join army. I begged him not to and I explained that if he did I would be back to living alone, and that I didn't want to move back in with his folks. But he said it was something he had to do and that everything would be okay, so he enlisted.

Meanwhile, I continued to work at the drugstore, but I decided to move to a nicer room in a different apartment building. One that was closer to my job.

He was stationed at Fort Dix, New Jersey and about once a month I would take a train to visit him there.

Those were fun times, except for one particular day. He talked me into getting into a cab with him and one of his buddies, and we headed for New York. I was excited because I had never been there before, but when we got there I learned that we were really only there because he wanted to look up an old girlfriend.

I was very hurt, however, his buddy was nice and offered to pay my way back to camp but I decided to stick it out. As the evening dragged on he got drunk and I was so mad I drank a double shot of whiskey, (straight.) Boy did that burn my throat. I thought, never again!

As he became more and more intoxicated we decided to get him to a restaurant, get some black coffee into him, and call a cab. With the help of a cab driver I was able to get him to Grand Central Station and get him on a train back to camp.

Once on the train he locked himself in the men's restroom and I had to get the conductor to get him out of there. I was embarrassed to be with him because he was attracting so much attention with his drunken behavior, acting up and cussing at everyone.

When we arrived back to the base the military police were waiting for him and they took him from the train and into custody. I begged and pleaded with them to go easy with him, telling them it was my fault that he was drunk and late getting back.

They seemed to believe me because all they really did was lecture him as they walked him away. I was afraid they were going to hurt him.

Not long after that he went AWOL again.

He came back to Cleveland and showed up at my apartment building while my dad was visiting me. He begged dad to loan him twenty dollars so he could get a bus ticket to Athens to see his folks and dad gave him the money. Then he left and hitchhiked down there and gave the money to his mother.

When he came back he found a piggy bank that I kept my tips in, smashed it on the floor, and took my money. When I asked him what he needed it for he said he had a date with a girl. He even told me her name. So a few days later I looked her address up and went to see her."

There is a theory shared by many that some girls who grow up in overly protective homes or in very strict environments sometimes gravitate to "**bad boys**."

Not so much a case of opposites being attracted to each other, but more likely because they represent something so different, even mysterious perhaps, that sometimes what were innocent and sheltered girls find something sexy or otherwise intriguing in the bad behavior of the guys wanting to control them.

They become willing to endure abusive behavior, even make excuses to others for not just the guy's bad behavior, but for themselves for staying in bad situations.

As a former police officer I used to see it all the time, and each time I did it was the same, no amount of counseling or advice meant anything to some of them.

Usually they would nod their head and mumble in agreement with me, but they would tag the conversation with excuses like, *I love him,* or, *it is not his fault that he is that way,* and sometimes they would blame themselves for his problems.

In many cases my efforts to suggest ways out of a bad relationship would be met by defiance and could even escalate into a bad predicament for me to be in. A few times while pulling a bully off someone I would have to defend myself from them both.

When we hear that police work can be a thankless job, these were some of the moments.

Sent often, sometimes repeatedly to the same home to find a beaten and bloodied victim waiting on the porch for us, begging us to leave her assailant, usually a husband or a boyfriend alone. Saying that he didn't mean it and that he only acted like that when he was drunk, and that in spite of his temper she still loved him and that she was sure he loved her.

And that if we really knew him, we might understand.

Probably not.

Some of these homes often smelled horrific and were cluttered with trash and their refrigerators were often empty. But they were willing to live in dumps like that with abusive men because they were *"in love."*

It always sickened me and left me wondering if maybe there is something to that theory about good girls and bad boys.

Maybe some girls will tolerate anything out of love or out of their discombobulated version of what that is. Love someone regardless of what they do to hurt them, break their spirit or their heart, they loved them.

"When I went to his girlfriend's house she wasn't there, but her mother was. She told me that her daughter had a son and that Bucky was the father, and that he promised to marry her for the sake of the baby. She told me that they had applied for a marriage license but that he left town before they could get married.

The woman was shocked to learn that he never left town and that he was already married to me.

A few days later he came home, and when I confronted him about what I had been told he became furious with me, he grabbed me by the throat and then slapped me in the face for going over there and then he tried to make a joke of it, saying the woman had lied to me.

Then when I started crying he tried to baby me, swearing that he loved me and promising that he would never do anything to hurt me, and that I should know that by now. When I reminded him of his violent temper and that he had just hurt me when he hit me in the face, he laughed and said "I barely touched you."

That night he was going to take me out to dinner but when we stepped out the door there were two M.P.'s waiting for him. They arrested him and took him back to Fort Dix. A few months later I received a collect call from California, it was him and he said he was on his way home.

He was AWOL again.

When he came back to Cleveland he said we needed to move, so we found an apartment on St. Clair Avenue, he joked that it was a "cold water flat" because it had no hot water.

One day his brother Dickie showed up for a visit and the landlord said we were not allowed to have company stay over, so Bucky got mad and he and Dickie left and went back to Athens.

I was left alone in that dingy apartment, so I invited my friend Marge Hynick over to spend the weekend. When the landlord found that out he evicted me.

I called my friend Marie and we decided to get an apartment together and share expenses. We found a nicer three-room place and I decided that since I was moving my address I might as well look for a new job closer to it.

Maybe that would make it more difficult for Bucky to find me. I was growing tired of all of his lies and deceit. And quite frankly I didn't think I could take the physical abuse any longer"

For the first time in Lillian's diary it sounds like she is finally waking up to the harsh reality that this guy isn't going to change.

Now sharing living quarters with a girlfriend she has known for years, someone she can trust and who is willing to contribute something to have a decent home and hopefully live in peace.

A place she hopes Bucky will not find, going as far as to even seek a new work-place, one she hopes he won't find.

Good for her if she means it.

One has to believe that Marie, a friend and likely confidant is probably not only comforting her and offering moral support, but surely she is encouraging her to get away from him and stay away. Marie, if not Lillian herself, has to be worried about her friend.

Maybe even herself, if Buck shows up knocking on their door.

In addition to just another job maybe she should try to find a completely different line of work. Every time she begins a new job behind some lunch counter, in a drug store or a hotel, he comes wandering through the door with new promises. After all, if he does not have her home address how many places like that can there be in downtown Cleveland?

Probably many but Bucky didn't seem to be too busy, he had time to look.

Moreover, he certainly had a motive, Lillian was his *baby doll*.

"My new job was in the drug store at the Allerton Hotel.

Shortly after I started working there Bucky showed up. He was acting sad and lonely and said he did not blame me for not wanting him around. He suggested that maybe our problem was that I didn't

*understand him, and that maybe it was his fault that he couldn't make
me understand why he was the way he was sometimes.*

*He said he was in town with nowhere to stay and he needed a
place to spend the night. Like a dummy I called Marie and asked if
she would mind if he slept at our place for just the night. She said she
didn't care so I gave him a key because I was working overnight.*

(Third shift.)

*When I got home the following morning he wasn't there. Neither
was my piggy bank that had contained $30.00, my share of the rent.
He had also taken my record player and pawned it.*

*About a week later he showed up again at work and apologized.
He promised that he would never hurt me again and that he would
change. He said that he had only stolen my money because he was in
a jam and had no other way out.*

I told him to get out.

Another entry into the diary that this apparent sleeping beauty is
finally getting the hint.

Maybe she is a little late in that regard but now her journal is
beginning to offer hope that she has figured this guy out, that his
promises are empty and that if she gives him even just one more
chance she will suffer further embarrassment or even worse, more
physical abuse.

However, Buck is an actor.

And a very good one it seems. We already know that he is a poet
and a conman, but can he continue to perform well and con his way
back into her heart forever, or is she finally getting it?

*"I thought when I threw him out of the drug store that maybe he
understood that I didn't want him around anymore, but the following
night he showed up again at my job. He had a bloody hand and when
I asked what had happened to him he said he had beaten some guy up
because he was saying nasty things about me.*

I again told him to get out.

*Later that night my landlady came in and told me that he had lied;
that he come to my apartment and when no one answered the door he
slammed his fist through a window.*

She said the police were looking for him.

He showed up at my apartment that night crying and I felt sorry for him and let him come in. I bandaged his hand and called a cab to take us to the emergency room.

When we got back home that night he was pleading with me to take him back and I was telling him I no longer wanted to know him. He started crying again and saying that if I did not take him back that he would jump off the High Level Bridge."

In another era, like the present one where there are better laws and more services available to protect people from domestic abusers, not to mention a society that is less tolerant or forgiving of men like Bucky, Lillian would have had a better chance of getting away from that madness and more importantly, staying away.

But this was the 1940s.

An era when wedding vows included a promise by women to honor and obey, and when it was almost unheard of for a man to be charged with abuses of any kind short of causing immediate medical attention for his victim.

Also a time when husbands could forcibly make wives have sex with them against their will, with barely a chance of being charged with rape. Where his home was his domain, or his castle, and when it was not unusual for wives to be expected to be subservient to them.

When domestic violence laws were vague at best, and too often not enforced, if at all in most cases.

Bucky knew this.

Love him or hate him, or probably both depending on the day or month, her story could get worse, and you can probably figure that it is about to. Because up to this point the challenge for Lillian has been her resolve to survive Buck's behavior personally. So far, until now at least, there are not any offspring to worry about.

If he were like this with his wife, what kind of father would he be if he were to become one?

"After he threatened to jump off a bridge if I left him I started feeling sorry for him and told him I would try one more time, but that I was sick of his deceit and of his overall meanness. He promised to do better and again, like a dummy I believed him.

It was 1948, I was twenty-three years old and pregnant, but he wasn't very thrilled about that.

Saying that we would need help, he coaxed me into going back to Athens and we moved in again with his folks in Sugar Creek. I spent most of my time stuck at home because I didn't drive and we were not close to anything, and besides I could not work because I was nearing the end of my pregnancy.

He on the other hand was spending most of his time in beer joints with his brothers and running around with other girls that he knew down there. As I have said before, I did like Dickie, he was always nice to me but Bucky was a bad influence on him.

One night I caught the two of them sneaking out of the house and I tried to follow them but I fell into a creek. Their mom and dad were watching from the porch and started laughing at me, even though I was pregnant.

No one came to help me.

Neither bothered to ask if I was okay, instead they laughed and ridiculed me. His mom kept saying that if I knew what was good for me I would leave Junior alone.

I was so mad.

He finally came home around 2:30, drunk and covered with lipstick. And when I told him about falling into the creek earlier that day, he too laughed and said, "That's what you get for not minding your own damn business."

The following morning he and Dickie woke up and headed for Nelsonville. I asked his brother Chad and a friend of his if the two could take me there to find them but they refused, "besides," his mother said, "If you try to find him he'll just beat you up again."

At this point I didn't care, I left anyway.

"After hitchhiking to Nelsonville I found them in a pick-up truck with two girls. When I confronted them Bucky got mad at me but he didn't beat me up. Instead he tried to apologize and convince me that I wasn't seeing what I thought I saw. He told me the girls were stranded and they were just about to give them a lift home.

A few days later a couple of M.P.s showed up and arrested him again. This time they had a trial and he was sentenced to two years in a military jail and would later be given a dishonorable discharge when he got out.

In the meantime I was stuck in Sugar Creek with his family.

My life was miserable."

No one but Lillian herself can know why she was *so* gullible, why she ever believed any of Bucky's lies about loving her or about changing his ways.   Reading her diary it is easy to blame her for allowing him to trick her into one misfortunate adventure after another. Moreover, it does seem to be an unexplainable mystery, why she did not do everything in her power to divorce him sooner than later.

But maybe she did.

It would be easy to assume that she thought about it, probably often. But remember this was more than sixty years ago. And although she managed to keep working, the jobs she held could not have paid much more than what was needed for basic survival let alone pay for an attorney, and she did not have the advantage of coming from a well grounded family who could lend their support. She didn't have a family port in a storm to go back to where she could live and save her money, and hopefully one day have enough to pay the legal fees necessary to free her from this life.

She was on her own.

A bigger mystery might be, where was her dad, or where was Hank?

Some of that is explained later, but in the meantime one real question is still there, how could she or anyone not related to Bucky through the DNA of his mother and father actually love him?

Unfortunately for her she did. Remember, this is still a love story, she was a woman still in love and still hoping for miracles.

"Buck Senior wasn't a bad guy, his son's needed to learn some manners, but the old man tried to be nice to me even though "Junior's" mom probably would have preferred he didn't. I was beginning to call him Junior like the others.

Lord please, don't let me become like them!

Bucky's sister Lovie was also kind to me, as was Dickie when he was not showing off for his big brother.

I truly believe that I only stayed alive for the day I could return to Cleveland!

I was receiving what was called an allotment from the army, ($50.00 each month) and I tried to put away, (hide) as much of that as I could so I would have money to take my baby back to Cleveland *after he was born. I was only a few days away from giving birth when one of Bucky's uncles began making inappropriate passes at me.*

He was repulsive and disgusting.

I was afraid to tell anyone else in the family because they weren't likely to care one way or another, or they may have blamed me somehow. Fearing they wouldn't believe me anyway, I kept it to myself.

Finally, on June 9, 1949 I began having labor pains around noon. I was home alone with Bucky's dad when my water broke around 4:30 in the afternoon. Even though he had seen this several times in his own large family he didn't know what to do so he ran out and returned with a neighbor, Ruth.

It was a Thursday, and after several attempts at trying to call for a squad one did eventually arrive. I was taken to Sheltering Arms Hospital and Bobby was born the following morning (Friday, June 10th) at 9:45 AM.

He was a beautiful baby!

Bobby 1949

Born with minor health issues, (Yellow Jaundice) I became very protective, but also very worried.

When I got him home I hovered over him as if he would break. I was afraid my in-laws might make him sicker than he was. Everything around him had to be sterilized and keeping his environment as clean as I had to wasn't easy in that dirty country home with almost no conveniences, and with so many people living in it.

However, within a few days Bobby pulled out of it and aside from who he was surrounded by he was fine. I wasn't sure how Bucky was going to react when he got out of the guardhouse.

What I did know was that I would not be sitting around in Athens with his family waiting for him. I had to go home. And six weeks after the baby was born I had enough money saved to do it.

I had $150.00 and I stuffed it into what was left of my so-called luggage, went next door and asked Ruth and her husband to drive me to the bus depot.

I was going home.

The bus pulled out of Athens around 9:30 that night, and at 12:30 AM it pulled into the bus terminal in Columbus. After a four-hour layover there we were back on the road and I was back in Cleveland at 9:30 in the morning.

Thank God!"

That four-hour layover in Columbus was something of an omen of things to come but Lillian didn't know it. After all it wasn't her first time there, and if she thought anything at all about where she was at that moment it may have only been of the brief period Bucky took her there to stay with his cousins.

Certainly not good memories, and maybe enough to make her glad when the bus got back on the road. She was focused on going home. Four hours in a bus terminal in downtown Columbus in July, 1949, not terribly significant.

Yet that is.

Probably thinking about the life she was running from and the people she was happy to leave behind, and probably relieved that she was only about 160 miles from home. Nevertheless, Columbus would one day become a city that would significantly change her life forever.

But for the good, or for worse?

"When the bus finally arrived in Cleveland I immediately went straight to my friend, Edna.

She had a two-room apartment and managed to talk her landlady into giving me a one-room housekeeping unit. It had a bed, a table, two chairs and a rocking chair that was perfect for rocking Bobby.

I took him to the welfare office and found that I qualified for $63.00 a month in assistance, as well as vouchers for free milk from the milkman every other day. That, along with my $50.00 a month army allotment was just enough for us to make it on, that is until Bobby was a little older and I could return to work.

He was a colic baby and I had to take him to the "Well Baby Clinic" downtown for his shots and examinations. I had bought him a baby bed to sleep in and a stroller to make it easier to take him with me on frequent trips to the clinic and on job searches".

With Buck still locked up and her in-laws all back in Athens, Lillian was in a safer place than she had been for a while. Her own apartment and learning to navigate the wellness system that helped struggling young single mothers, or mothers left in single circumstances, and she wasn't working anywhere so if Bucky or his relatives did come to town it wouldn't be as easy be to find her.

She was home, reconnecting with old friends and getting on with life as a new mother. For the first time in her own life she was the guardian of someone else.

Her own foster homes and a life dictated by someone else's rules behind her, she was learning on her own how to care for another human being. To be responsible for a child's food and shelter as well as his health and well being. Where she lived would now be her choice. That is unless Bucky would return with other ideas.

After all, she was never able to resist him in the past.

"When Christmas rolled around Bobby was six months old and we got our first Christmas tree. I decorated it with tinsel and angel hair, and it was very pretty. I was so proud of it.

Bucky was able to learn from the army where I lived by tracing the address the allotment check was being mailed to. I received a letter from them advising that he was being discharged from the service and that money would no longer be coming to me, but he would be.

It might be hard to understand but I was actually excited about him coming and meeting his new son.

Bobby was six months old and he had never even seen a picture of him, I was sure he would be proud, and I wanted everything to be perfect when he came. On the day he was due in Cleveland I had Bobby all cleaned up and dressed in his best baby clothes, he was so cute.

When Bucky got there he wasn't that excited about the baby, he treated Bobby okay but the first thing he wanted to do was get a baby-sitter so he and I could go out and celebrate his homecoming. I was nervous about allowing someone else to watch Bobby because I hadn't left him with anyone before. I insisted that wherever we went we would have to take him.

So Bucky went out alone, and when he came home we decided that we should live together and try to make our family work.

What else could I have done? I needed help and Bobby needed a daddy.

So he moved in, and for a few days everything was okay but he didn't like my friend Edna and it bothered him that she lived next door.

He used that as an excuse to start running around again and drinking heavily, and each time he did he would come home in a mean mood and take it out on Bobby and me. And after being beaten around he would always try to cuddle up to me and pour on the charm, always promising that was the last time.

I can't put it into any words that anyone would ever understand, but I still loved him and I agreed to go back to Athens with him, with the promise that things would be better this time."

No surprise that Buck was not starting out well as a new father or that after seeing him for the first time he immediately left and went out to celebrate, not that he had a son, but because he was again away from the military and free do as he pleased.

Nor is his behavior a surprise following his release from the service after serving two years in lock-up, he came out just as he went in. After two failed stints in the United States armed forces he still was not showing any signs of maturity, let alone the responsibility of being a parent.

Maybe he wasn't anymore cut out to be a dad than he was a husband.

Just a guess.

"Back in Athens I learned I was pregnant again but Bucky wasn't very thrilled about it and neither were his folks. So he decided we should move to Columbus. We found a housekeeping room on Bryden Road and he got a job working for Isaly's Ice Cream Store.

He bought Bobby a stroller and me a very pretty electric clock with a figure of a horse on it.

But not much more changed. He was staying out late every night, claiming that he was working, but that turned out to be more lies.

One evening he came home from work and made me wash a white shirt for him, (I washed all of our clothes on a washboard in the sink in those days) then he got dressed up, shined his shoes and said he had to go to a meeting.

I didn't believe him so I took Bobby out to the car, got in and just sat there. I knew that he didn't have any kind of job that would require meetings at night, and besides, I reminded him that he had promised to take Bobby and me to the drive-in movies.

So he got in, started the car and drove us around the block, then came back and parked in front of our apartment building and got out. Then he went inside and came back with the baby stroller, snatched Bobby from me, sat him in the stroller and said, "There is, take care of him."

Then he pulled me out of the car, jumped in, and drove off.

He didn't come back home until around 2:30 in the morning, drunk and smelling like perfume and with lipstick all over his shirt. When I said something to him about it he pushed me aside, went to bed and told me to leave him alone. I knew that tone of voice and I knew that I had better just let it go.

He did this a lot, and each time he did I was left feeling lonely and depressed but it never seemed to matter to him. I wanted to get away but I was pregnant and I had an eleven-month-old baby to take care of. I didn't know what else I could do but stay and hope for better days.

Bobby was all I had to take my mind off the things that kept me feeling helpless. I remember I would take him for long walks in his stroller just for something to do. Bucky would never allow me to try to make friends or go out without him.

Living in Columbus was not like home for Lillian, she missed the friendlier confines of her native Cleveland every day but was still glad to be away from Buck's family and out of Athens, even though she got along well with his sisters.

One of them, Sara had become very sympathetic to her, often trying to step between Buck and his abusive behavior, and she and Lillian would remain close for decades. She was the only one in that entire family that Lillian remained close to.

"In September, 1950 we moved back to Athens but right away Bucky kept coming up with reasons why he needed to return to Columbus.

Every weekend.

I learned that he had a girlfriend there and he blamed Sara for telling me. He told her to "mind her own damn business." He had the foulest mouth on any man I had ever known. I found out that he had given Bobby's stroller to that girl for her baby, as well as my piggy bank and a stuffed bunny I had bought for Bobby. With him gone a lot I was stuck with his folks in Milfield.

(Another town in Athens County.)

On October first, while having dinner I was doubling over with labor pains. Bucky and his mother both thought it was funny and were making jokes about it, but his Aunt Lucille knew it was serious and she insisted that he take me to see a doctor.

They took me to a country doctor they knew but he wasn't there, his wife said he was playing golf and she didn't know when he would return, so we left a message for him to come to the house as soon as possible and we came back home.

At around 8:35 that night Patty was born at home. She was a beautiful baby!

When she was two weeks old Bucky came home and found me quarreling with his brother Chad and he grabbed me by the hair, dragged me outside, started choking me and then kicked me in the stomach.

It seemed that he was becoming more and more abusive, and most of his family was always taking his side, especially his mother.

When Patty was five weeks old I packed up both babies and what I could carry and went back to Cleveland. Another ride on a Greyhound Bus, another long layover in Columbus, and when I finally got back into Cleveland I had very little money so I took a room at the Allison Hotel for two dollars a day.

I made a bed for Patty in a dresser drawer and Bobby slept with me. I was able to take their baby bottles down to the hotel restaurant where a kind waitress would warm their milk."

Patty 1950

These were hard times, not just for Lillian's seemingly unending marital miseries, but it was an era where simple modern comforts and conveniences just were not always available to her.

Imagine all of those trips back and forth from Cleveland to Athens on buses that didn't have air-conditioning, living in rooms she refers to as *housekeeping rooms* and hotel rooms, some without means to cook and some without hot water. Rooms that were sometimes managed by cranky landlords who dictated who could come or go. Then imagine this city girl being dumped out in the country to live with a family that not only didn't want her there, but with a few horny in-laws trying to take advantage of her, and a mother-in-law who delighted in heckling her and reinforcing her abuser.

Moreover, the different homes those people lived in.

They were poor country folks living in houses that could not have been comfortable, especially for a young pregnant woman and especially during hot summer months.

This was also the era before television.

Most likely there was a radio in the house, probably tuned into a station that played what was commonly called **Hillbilly Music** then and as Lillian would say in later years, she never cared for that stuff.

After all, she grew up in Jewish homes in a big city, probably hearing polite orchestra music or when she could, the Big Bands and ballads she loved. But there was the country music, probably on all the time. And as she listened to songs about lost loves, broken lives, drinking and raising hell she was hearing constant reminders of where she was. Probably identifying with all of the pain and emotions these songs were about. Like being kicked in the heart, she might have looked at that radio and thought, *"if you only knew."*

It is no wonder she wasn't a big fan of that stuff.

Imagine that.

Living out in the country or as she described it, *being far away from civilization* with very little money, no real friends, hoping no one tries to abuse you and spending most days and nights bored to death and feeling sorry for yourself. And with the sad truth of knowing that you put yourself there because you believed you were in love?

Imagine being a non-smoker sharing close living quarters with several people who all smoke, and a non-drinker in a home with several who do anytime they have enough money to buy alcohol, some who when after having had too many pose a physical threat.

And we can only guess what nutrition was like, what was available in homes short on cash and long on needs by the numbers of them who crowded together. What sort of diet might have been available for Lillian during her pregnancies and with only a country doctor nearby, who if he was not at home or was difficult to find, what sort of prenatal care did she receive?

Probably none, even minor illnesses probably had to be ridden out.

Stomach aches, common colds and headaches may have had to run their course. Imagine being pregnant with no indoor plumbing and that many people at home to share an outhouse.

Then imagine doing all of that with the responsibility of caring for a couple of babies and having to keep their clothing and diapers clean when your only means to wash them is a scrub board. Being a young attractive woman having to hitchhike along dusty country roads alone when there was no one around to take you places you needed to go or when there wasn't enough money for taxicabs or busses, if you could even get one.

And finally, imagine getting where you want to go and trying to navigate a public assistance program in 1950. All of this would be extremely difficult now, but what was it like in an era when there wasn't much in the way of social networking or for people who could not show a permanent address, or for anyone naïve to the system in general.

Difficult times for anyone, but even harder for someone trying to outrun a physically and mentally abusive spouse.

But was Lillian really trying to outrun Bucky or just trying to stay ahead of him long enough to catch her breath? Knowing all along that no matter how far or how fast she ran he would catch up and pull her back into his world.

I believe that deep inside she knew this man was not worth the loving feelings she was wasting on him, I also believe that if she was certain that she could get him out of her life and keep him out that she would have.

Nevertheless, I have to wonder if after all of those beatings, both verbally and physically if she was scared to death of him. Perhaps taking him back all of those times out of fear of what he might do if she didn't, especially after she became a mother.

After all, she never did have a great protector in her own life.

Her own parents seemed to have abandoned their responsibilities when she was not much older than a toddler. The foster families who took care of her may have done so only because they were paid to by the child welfare organization in Cuyahoga County.

That wouldn't have been too uncommon then. There is not much evidence here that very many people worried about her safety, ever. Police officers maybe, but even they cannot help if they are unaware of the dangers, and not even they could be around all the time or even the times they were needed.

As a former cop I used to answer the question…*"Where is a cop when you need one?"* with…*"If we were there you wouldn't need us."*

Tough guys aren't too tough when someone who is capable of stopping them is close by, but Lillian, like so many other victims of spousal abuse did not call them as often as she should have, I doubt that she even had access to a phone when help was needed most.

According to her diary she never called them.

What she needed more than anything else in the world was someone who would show up in her life like a knight in shining armor. One who would sweep her off her feet and to send a message to Bucky that she was no longer an easy mark, left to fend for herself.

And who would take care of not only her but take on the responsibility of parenting another man's children. Where would someone like that come from? Would someone like that *ever* show up, and if he did would she be willing to let him into her life?

"One day while going down to the hotel restaurant I bumped into an old boyfriend. (Bob Hatfield.)

He was a doll!

We sat and talked about the old days and how we once cared for each other, and what our lives would be like had we stayed together.

And he asked me to leave Bucky.

He said he would take care of the kids and me. However, I was married to Bucky, I was the mother of his children and I could not make myself believe that divorcing him was really the right thing to do.

I let him get away again.

My next move was to apply for welfare assistance, but I was told I did not qualify because I was not a "permanent resident" of Cuyahoga County. Then I applied to the Soldiers and Sailors Relief organization, the Red Cross and the Salvation Army for help, all without success.

Soon after that Bucky showed up begging me to take him back and promising me that he had changed. As a peace offering he had brought a snowsuit for Bobby.

Once again I believed him and we found a housekeeping room in a boarding house.

He found a job at a bowling alley that paid $10.00 a night. Not long after that he quit his job and talked me into moving back to Milfield.

There, I got a job at the Home Restaurant and Bucky's sister Lovie agreed to baby-sit the kids while I went to work. I had to walk the two miles to work every day because Bucky was again back to his old ways, always gone when I needed him.

After several fights, mostly about his drinking and running around with other women, I decided that I had finally had enough. I was going to leave him for good this time, so I packed what I could and took the kids back to Cleveland.

I found a job at the London Grille as a waitress, while a neighbor woman babysat every day for me. I was meeting some very nice people at work; one particular fellow began showing me a lot of interest and was constantly asking me out. Once he even left me a $50.00 tip, it was a fifty-dollar bill!

It was later stolen."

This is textbook; taken straight out of Lillian's life story, taking one-step forward and two steps back. She cannot catch a break and when there is a hint that she is on the cusp of a better life or at least a chance of it she either doesn't recognize it or she is too stubborn to admit that Buck is a dead end.

That none of his promises have a bottom, or that it is plainly obvious that there are no new leaves for him to turn over. In her case love was not only blind, it stifled common sense.

Love, or whatever her emotions for him were was clearly her worst enemy. And with two kids coming as a package deal for anyone who might want to wrap his arms around her life, and more and more time going by, any such likelihood of being rescued from that miserable life was probably becoming less and less.

Not to say that she was getting closer to passing her prime as an attractive woman, she was still a young good-looking twenty-six year old woman, but she was packing two kids and a troublesome past that included a bad penny that keeps coming back like a rusted boomerang.

Bucky!

"For Bobby's second birthday I had saved enough money to buy him a tricycle and just when I was doing well on my own Bucky showed up. More promises about having changed, pouting about being lonely and saying everything I wanted him to say to make me believe that maybe we could work it out. That maybe we could be a family and that Bobby and Patty could actually grow up with their daddy.

That is what I wanted to believe.

But he didn't want me working at the London Grille so I quit and went to work for my old friend Gus at the Blossom Restaurant. My hours were from 11:00 PM until 7:00 AM. Bucky was supposed to be babysitting but I found out that he was leaving the kids home alone and running in and out of beer joints all night. He said that he would quit that lifestyle if I would move back to Milfield with him, so I again fell for his lies."

It is as if this man had complete control over her mind and could continue making her believe in the impossible. That his personality would one day change and that he would eventually get his priorities straight or care about anything but himself. All of that from a man whose only attributes were his good looks and his ability to sweet-talk his way in and out of things, a man who she often described as an egomaniac.

(Ya think!)

Someone who considered himself *God's gift to women,* and actually saying those words about himself, sometimes to her when trying to explain his infidelity as he primped and dressed to go out on her and with enough arrogance to tell her where he was going.

The guy had some sort of hypnotic way of convincing her that no matter how deplorable and disgusting his behavior was, that his good looks somehow made keeping him around worth it.

Worth the lies, the physical abuse and the humiliation she went through time after time. He was like some sort of bad drug that took over any ability for her to think rationally.

On Patty's first birthday Bucky and Chad said they were going to a junkyard in Nelsonville, and Bobby wanted to go with them. When he climbed into the back seat of the car Basil made him get out. As they sped away the car kicked up gravel and dust all over us, and Bobby was crying because he was left behind.

I felt so sorry for him.

He and his brother had both been drinking heavily that day and shortly after they left a neighbor came over and told me that they had been in a terrible accident. Their car had rolled over several times, and was demolished; they were both in the hospital in Nelsonville. He had a broken leg among other injuries and Chad had a broken arm.

For once he had done the right thing by making Bobby get out of that car and I thanked God for that. It was probably the only time in my life I ever thanked God for something he did.

He was taken from his hospital room by State Troopers and put in the Nelsonville jail for driving drunk that day".

It was October 1st, and I was pregnant again.

When he went to court the judge sentenced him to several days in jail and told him that he needed that cast more on his head than on his leg. While he was locked up his dad drove me to see him every day to take him food, cigarettes and coffee.

That stay in jail seemed to make him meaner than when he went in because when he did come home he was awful. Once he chased me out of the house and when he couldn't catch me- because of the cast on his leg, he threw his crutch at me. When it missed hitting me that made him even madder, he was out there cussing me and threatening to hurt me even worse if I didn't come back.

After he got his cast off we moved to Columbus and found a two-room apartment.

I got a job at Pete's Coney Island on South High Street but Pete only allowed me to work until I was five months pregnant. Two weeks after I quit, two Columbus Police detectives showed up at our apartment and arrested Bucky. They said he had stolen two checks from Pete and forged them. I begged Pete to let me work two weeks without pay (which I did) in exchange for dropping the charges. He agreed to let me, and Bucky was released.

That meant nothing to him, a few days later I found him in a beer joint with a seventeen-year-old girl and when I told him he was needed at home with his kids he went into a rage and tore my blouse. That night he took the girl to Lancaster and was arrested for something down there and put back in jail.

He called me collect (on our landlady's phone) and begged me to come down and bail him out."

Bucky, Bobby and Patty 1952

The word is *enabling*.

All of this could have been over for Lillian had she admitted to herself long before that Buck was not going to change. He knew that regardless of how bad he treated those around him, especially her, that he would be forgiven and given more opportunities to abuse everyone around him, neglect his children and steal from anyone he could, not to mention his many romantic indiscretions with whoever else he could tag as an easy get.

And he got many, and he didn't care who knew, often bragging about his infidelity even to Lillian. He would even blame her for the abuse by saying that his problems and poor choices in life were because of her. In addition, at the end of those baseless arguments he would snicker and go off into his own fantasy world where he would again get into more trouble, time after time and expect her or someone else to run to his aid, and someone always did.

She did that too many times if she did it twice.

Reading her story it is difficult to not grit ones teeth or pound on a table as if we could change something. Maybe change the next line in her diary where we know she is going to run back to Cleveland and he is going to sweet talk her back to Athens, or the one that begins to talk about some drunken fit that leads to beating her up, breaking something or giving away or selling her things.

And although I do want to pound that table and shake my head at the unbelievable way she allows herself to be duped time and again I have to believe that somewhere deep inside of that abused woman's mind that she actually believed that better days would come. Still believing in miracles, either that or she simply grew to accept the cards she had been dealt.

Yes, that hand sucked but it is never too late or too soon to throw in a rotten hand and ask for a new deal.

As the narrator of this diary I am finding it a lesson in futility. One that I got very used to as a police officer. Waiting for sure signs… no make that hoping to read a convincing passage that she will awaken from what seems like some sort of weird deep sleep, one that seems more like a coma.

Clearly she seems unable to rationalize with good basic common instincts, like a victim of some mysterious form of brainwashing in addition to everything else. As I mentioned before her misery went beyond Buck's infidelity and abuse, now pregnant again with two other babies to care for and suffering again through another very hot summer.

Still getting slapped around and trying to reason with a man who seems incapable of such things. And as the narrator I am hoping at this point that the next line in her diary says something like, *"No, I am not coming to Lancaster to bail your sorry ass out. Stay there and rot for all I care.)*

That is what I had hoped to see.

"Dumb me, I dressed Bobby and Patty and hitchhiked to Lancaster. When the judge saw me, pregnant and with two babies he felt sorry for me and excused Bucky's bail. He told him to take the twenty-five dollars and buy his kids some groceries.

That night he was back in the beer joints.

But he did go looking for a job a few days later. He didn't find one but he at least made the effort. Or so he said.

A few nights' later (July 25, 1952) I was at home, when my water broke. We were living on South Fifth Street near Livingston Avenue in the south end at the time, and Bucky was actually home that night. He took me to the Ohio State University Hospital where at 3:18 AM, July 26-Ricky, a beautiful baby with very blond fuzzy hair was born. When he was three weeks old we moved to Detroit."

Ricky 1952

With three kids now in tow, two babies and a toddler it may seem odd that their destination would be Detroit Michigan. In the past the road went back to Athens County, or to Cleveland and *then* back to Athens.

As the family continued to add new members maybe Buck was just ready for a change of scenery, or maybe Lillian was finally able to convince him that she could no longer follow him up and down those same roads to nowhere.

It was bad enough that she was repeatedly enabling his irresponsible and abusive behavior by always allowing him to sweet talk her into one nightmare after another, but following him back or being drug back to *the hills* was almost a certain guarantee of more of the same for her, and for the children. Constantly expected to live with the chaos that surrounded his dysfunctional family, one that seemed to have very little of anything and who seemed content, even preferring to live with one another regardless of the hardships they brought onto themselves.

Still, there had to be a reason why Buck would be willing to trade Athens for Detroit, and it probably wasn't because there was a job waiting for him there and in all likelihood probably not because he was ready to turn over a new leaf.

"My dad had gotten us a place to stay, and it didn't cost us anything. It was a small housekeeping room but it was clean and it was a home. Ricky was so tiny that I made a bed for him in a dresser drawer. In addition dad promised to help us out financially."

Oh.

Okay, so therein lies the incentive to go north instead of south. But if Buck doesn't find a job, and if he continues his selfish ways and keeps making bad decisions such as drinking too much and ignoring his responsibilities, or breaking laws including the ones relating to domestic violence then his father-in-law's gesture of good-will probably should have been extended to only his daughter and his grandchildren.

"One day Bucky told me he needed me to wake him up early in the morning because he had found a job. But I overslept and while I was rushing around to help him get ready for work I fractured my foot.

He became furious and refused to take me to see a doctor, so my dad called a cab to take me there.

(Dad didn't drive because of his bad eyesight.)

I wound up with a cast on my leg and had to hobble around on crutches and that too made him mad. Always complaining because I couldn't move fast enough for him, heckling me for my predicament and calling me names and just being his usual mean self. However, he did actually find a job in a restaurant, and with the little bit of extra money we were able to move into a bigger apartment.

But dad still felt sorry for us, so he found us a house.

The price of it was $9,500.00 and he put $900.00 down. The monthly mortgage payment was $65.00, but he told us that we would only have to pay $40.00 of that along with half of the utilities if he could stay with us. Bucky agreed and I finally felt like my life of living in one-room housekeeping units and drafty, smelly old country houses was changing for the better. Maybe those days were finally over.

It was a very pretty home.

We had seven rooms, a bath, basement, attic, a nice yard and even a garage. The first thing Bucky did was buy a car to park in it. It was a Kaiser. Then he went out and bought some furniture for the home, on payments of course. And of course, signing my name beside his.

But I really thought that things were changing and that everything would finally be okay. We were a real family, in a real home. It was good, and I thought that everything was going to be at least better."

A home, a real one as Lillian called it.

A place where she could now feel safe and could begin planning a future with the closest thing she ever had to a real family with five out the six people sharing four walls and a roof as well as DNA.

And of course, Buck.

Twenty seven years old with three children safely docked in real bedrooms with real beds and under the watchful eyes of not only a working husband, but of a father who seems ready to play the role and actually be there for moral as well as financial support.

It was good, but was everything really going to stay that way?

"Soon after we settled in and when things began falling into place Bucky began running around and was drinking heavily, more than

in the past. He was getting meaner and he kept complaining about missing his folks, about living with dad and how unhappy he was.

He refused to help with any of the bills, he would not buy any groceries and he broke his promise to help dad with the house payments so I found a job in a restaurant. I would bring home things like bread, milk, hot chocolate, eggs and sometimes sandwiches, and I would give dad whatever was left over to help out with the expenses, that is, whatever I could hide from Bucky.

When I confronted him about running around, drinking and refusing to contribute any money to the family he broke a chair over my head. My dad was mad and very hurt but he was no match physically to prevent him from doing things like that. But he got me into a cab and took me to the emergency room.

After that incident the two of them stopped talking to each other, which made for a very uncomfortable home.

One day Bucky decided we should leave and move back to Columbus. When we told my dad he was very upset but said that he would keep the house for six months in case I changed my mind, but only if I came home without Bucky. Poor dad, I should have sent Bucky back to Columbus by himself and stayed in Detroit to help him.

That would have avoided future heartbreaks."

Probably many, not to mention further physical violence and a continuum of financial nightmares and only more of what she had known as his wife, insurmountable challenges and more hell.

At this stage Detroit sounds like a pretty good town to live in.

Buck heading south, and Lillian contemplating staying in Michigan with her dad and her kids, sounds good for everyone. But we know better, even though Columbus has never had anything good to offer her in the past we know that her dad will be selling that house in six months. And why Columbus, wouldn't Cleveland be closer?

After all, it is just on the other side of Lake Erie.

The old girlfriend perhaps.

The state capitol is becoming something of the new Cleveland for Lillian; it may one day not only become her permanent home but where her life comes to an eventual end.

"As we were preparing to move back to Columbus, he sold our furniture for $150.00, even though it wasn't paid for. We moved in with some of his family who had come up from Athens.

They were renting a place in the north end on East Como Avenue and at least fifteen of them were living there, we made twenty. Even Bucky felt crowded, and I was miserable being surrounded by that many people, especially that many of his rowdy relatives! So we found a two-room housekeeping unit on North Starr Avenue, but the landlord only allowed two kids so we snuck Ricky in.

He was six months old.

I got a job at The Campus Neil Restaurant across from University Hospital and Bucky would frequently ask me to get a pay advance against my check, which always left me short on payday.

I worked the night shift and when I got off at one o'clock in the morning I had to walk home.

His brother Dickie was very ill at the time and was in the hospital (University) and I would visit him every day. I really liked him because of all of the brothers he was the only one who ever respected me or was willing to stand up to Bucky when he was being mean to me or the kids.

Sadly, he died in that hospital in February, 1953. Strange, that Ricky who we named after him was born there just seven months before that.

That summer we were in Athens visiting his mom and dad when the police showed up with a warrant for his arrest. He had stolen some furniture from some other relatives and they filed charges against him. After he was taken to jail I had had it!

Again.

I headed back to Columbus to look up some friends I had made there, and one of them offered to allow me and the kids to stay with her in Lincoln Park. I didn't want to go back to the north end where I knew he would come looking for us when he was released from jail."

Lillian and kids, Lincoln Park

Lincoln Park, or *the projects* as it was known was on the south side of Columbus a few blocks east of Parsons Avenue. To describe it politely it was slightly above a dead end for single-mothers, many of whom like Lillian had either been married or were living with abusive men and their kids. It was a group of subsidized apartments built in the 1940s to house military families. Small cramped buildings separated by narrow alleyways with little to no conveniences, and with indoor floors and staircases made of concrete and steel.

Many women like Lillian did their laundry at a nearby Laundromat or on washboards in washtubs or sinks, hanging it to dry on clotheslines sometimes hung outside or stretched across a room inside. Many if not most relied on others for basic transportation, it was likely that very few of them could have afforded to own a car anyway.

Lillian would come to rely on charitable organizations such as the Salvation Army for clothing for her and her kids, the Southeast Lions Club for Ricky's glasses. He was born with crossed eyes and would need corrective surgery before he was three years old.

In the winters they would receive their coats from an organization called Charity Newsies.

And in an era before food stamps or government issued cards to purchase basic store brand groceries she received vouchers for products labeled *U.S. Government Commodities.* Food like powdered eggs and powdered milk, packaged in brown or gray paper containers marking what was inside, or glass jars and tin cans similarly identified. In addition, there was a school on the complex grounds where she could enroll her children, along with the hundreds of other rag-a-muffins growing up there.

Lillian in Lincoln Park

"While staying with my friends I filled out an application for my own apartment in Lincoln Park. Meanwhile I found a job at Zanes Grille as a waitress. My hours there were 10:30 AM until 7:00 PM, and I paid my friend $9.00 a week to baby-sit.

One night I came home and saw my friend's her husband beating her and I immediately ran upstairs to check the kids. They were okay but scared.

I continued pressing at the apartment office for my own place and with the help of a man I had met at work, Jim Blake we got our own place. Jim was a very nice man who helped the kids and me a lot. He was almost like a dad to me.

On the weekend when we got our apartment I was feeling bad about Bucky being in jail so I made the mistake of packing up the kids and buying a Greyhound Bus ticket to Athens to visit him. Bobby was four years old, Patty was three and Ricky was 14 months old. Can you imagine toting three babies more than seventy miles on a hot bus only to find out when we got there that we could not see him?

He was in isolation for bad behavior.

I remember that it was so hot and sticky that day. I had my hands full with three fussy babies and I wasted not just our time, but precious money to travel down there. I was wondering all the way home, "When will I ever get a break!"

Maybe that was a break.

I mean, traveling all the way to Athens, much of the way along dusty country roads on a hot bus in the summer of 1954 was a miserable way to spend an entire day, but not being allowed to visit Buck was far from the worst thing that ever happened to her on those journeys back down Route 33.

At least this time she did not have to stay there for an extended period, and this time she had her own home to come back to. One that was away from the lifestyle he would have locked her up in.

But there were other issues back in Lincoln Park that she was worried about. Issues such as trying to keep her kids properly clothed and fed, keeping a roof over their heads and keeping them away from dangerous people, some who lived within the projects as well as outsiders who frequented the area seeking to take advantage of vulnerable people down on their luck, a problem that has plagued low-income communities forever.

Bobby, Ricky and Patty in Lincoln Park

Lillian in Lincoln Park

The kids in 1954

"Things were as good as I could make them for me and the kids. Our apartment wasn't in the best area, but it was clean and we had what we absolutely needed. Not much more, but what we needed to survive. Four walls around us and a roof over our heads to keep us safe, and it was just us.

My earnings as a waitress weren't much, but occasionally I received decent tips, but paying for babysitting was making it more and more difficult to just get by. Considering the other expenses I had to pay, like utility bills, lunch money for the kids, gas money if we needed to be taken somewhere, or even something simple like change once in awhile for the ice-cream bike that peddled through the alleys each day so the kids wouldn't always feel left out.

All of that in addition to worrying about their basic health, and their safety. My friend's husband was not the nicest man around either, he was a heavy drinker like Bucky with a personality to match, he was an angry man most of the time, yelling and screaming a lot, and I didn't like it that my kids had to see that every day.

But I didn't know many people in Lincoln Park at the time, or at least anyone else I could have trusted to take care of them while I worked so I decided to quit my job, stay home with the kids and ask for assistance. I was accepted into a program called Aid for Dependent Children, (ADC) which qualified me for $116.00 a month in assistance. After paying my rent, that left $92.00 a month for everything else.

In November of that year I learned that Bucky's trial was set to take place just before Thanksgiving. I took the kids back down to Athens hoping for the best for him, hoping that he would be released and at least try to help me and the kids, or to just come home and behave like a normal person, but the judge sentenced him to one year in prison."

After all of the torment- and years of abuse and neglect, Lillian was still hoping that a side of Buck he had yet to show would somehow emerge, that there was some chance that he could change. Maybe believing that he was learning valuable lessons by being locked up and deprived of his freedom, not to mention an opportunity to share a life with someone who not only cared for him but who was always willing to forgive his many indiscretions.

It was the holiday season and another one that would require the generosity of others to make it seem so.

"It was our first Christmas in Lincoln Park and Jim had gotten us a Christmas tree while Mrs. Bauer, a social worker arranged for presents for the kids. We even received a basket of food collected by students at nearby South High School.

It was a very nice Christmas for us after all.

I was making friends with some very nice people, and the kids seemed to be adapting as well.

Still, I felt that Bucky should at least be able to see his kids, so whenever possible I would dress them up and hitch a ride to take them to the London Correctional Institute for visits. I would tell them that they were going to visit daddy at his army base, I didn't want them to know he was in prison.

When his sentence was almost up and it was time for his parole I went before the parole board and spoke on his behalf. In order to be released he had to prove that he had a home to go to, (I had the home) and he needed to have a job.

He had to promise to change his ways and take care of his family and he had to promise his parole officer that he would keep the job he found for him with the Priestas Brothers who owned a garage building company.

When he was paroled he came to live with me and the kids in our small apartment, then he immediately tried to move some of his relatives in with us as well, into that tiny apartment that was barely big enough for the five of us. When his mother and several members of his family showed up I couldn't afford to feed them all. I had to ask for an emergency grocery order from welfare because he wanted to prepare a banquet for them to celebrate his release from prison.

Poor Bobby was not feeling well that day and was asking for oatmeal so I asked Bucky if he would fix it for him but he blew up and told me to fix it myself, then he threw a cup of hot coffee in my face.

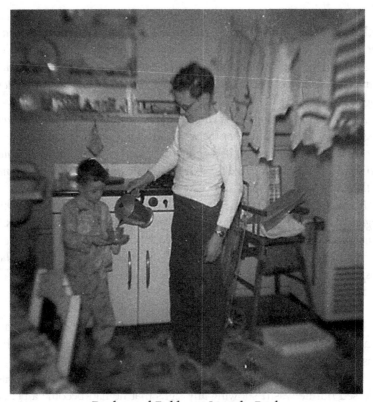

Bucky and Bobby at Lincoln Park

Incarceration is supposed to accomplish two things; one, it is punishment for breaking laws, and two it is hoped that by depriving people of their basic civil liberties and freedom that they will return to polite society better people than they were before they were locked up. Better behaved and less likely to repeat the offenses that got them locked away from the rest of the world in the first place. Perhaps realize the errors of their previous miserable ways and hopefully change them.

Maybe even be grateful to those who are willing to take them in and give them a second chance to get it right. Or a third, or as many as it takes. Buck would surely need more than a few because after all, he promised that he would change his ways several times in the past but never did, and now he had very good reasons to but was he able to see it that way?

"It didn't take long for him to go back to his old ways. He forged a check and used it to buy himself a car. In addition to the down payment that was not any good in the first place he forged my signature as a cosigner for the balance of the loan. When he brought the car home Patty who was four years old tried to get in and she accidentally slammed the car door on her finger.

As she was screaming and crying in pain he went into a rage and began cussing her out and calling her the worst possible names. Then he ordered her inside and made her sit in a chair in the corner, for being as he said "so stupid!" When I protested the way he was treating her, he punched me in the face.

My dad was visiting at the time and tried to comfort Patty but Bucky began screaming at him, telling him to "mind his own damn business." A neighbor and a friend of mine, Mary Tackett came over and bandaged Patty's finger because he would not allow anyone to take her to the hospital.

He said we couldn't afford it."

Being grateful to those willing to help an ex-con, or given second chances to get it right did not seem to be lessons Buck learned while he was doing time in prison.

The circumstances were in place for him to stay out of jail after he was released but he wasn't showing any signs that he had become a better person or that he understood the conditions of his parole. Even though he was provided a home and someone was willing to give him a break by hiring him to work, there was still nothing about him suggesting any hint of rehabilitation.

Going to and serving time in prison was only punishment for a small fraction of his previous offenses, but did any of that experience teach him anything at all? Were there any signs that new leaves might now be turned over, or that he would ever appreciate the opportunity to not only be free, but would he assume the responsibility of raising and nurturing the kids he fathered?

Being so aggravated by a request to feed his son some oatmeal- that he threw hot coffee into his wife's face then punched her. Or screaming at his young daughter and calling her names, and even punishing her for accidentally closing a car door on her finger and refusing to seek medical attention for her does not suggest an improvement in parenting skills.

Writing a bad check to buy a car, well…

"Bucky was arrested again.

This time for stealing checks from his employer, the Priestas Brothers, and forging them. He was convicted of forgery and sent back to London.

He accused me of calling the law on him but not only did I not I call them then, I never called them, ever. Not even when I was on the receiving end of his beatings, or when he stole from my dad, or from my employers or me.

When the police or a deputy sheriff showed up those times it was either because they had a warrant for his arrest or because neighbors would call when they heard screams, or glass and furniture being broken.

But I was blamed nonetheless.

While he was back I prison his uncle Val started hanging around Lincoln Park. He was constantly flirting with me and asking me to get a divorce and run off with him. I could not stand the sight of that man.

When I complained to Lovie about him she brought her boyfriend and her brother Chad over and they beat him severely with a pipe. Even after that I had to file charges against him for something else and he was arrested and put in jail.

He was a vulgar and disgusting man.

With some of the problems plaguing Lillian's life locked away for the time being, she found time to meet and date a few *nicer* guys. She was beginning to understand, or if not that, at least accept the possibility that life with this family would never improve. That the man she loved was not much of a man and wasn't likely to ever become much of one.

She was lonely and feeling deprived of anything that resembled a normal life. Feeling sorry for herself and surrendering to the reality that her childhood was the happiest time of her life.

How could that possibly make sense?

As a child she was moved from one foster home to another where she was often used as a maid, she barely knew her own mother, was often neglected by her father and would sometimes be locked up in detention facilities for menial things. And to cap that happy time she had to quit school and get a job to pay room and board to a foster family when she was only in the tenth grade.

What a sad reality to have to think of that as one's happiest times.

Not much was written about her brother Hank and where he was during her post-foster care; however, it is known that he was so eager to put his own childhood struggles behind him that at sixteen he ran away and joined the navy. There he learned a trade in electronics and following his military service he would eventually move to Arizona and become a successful businessman owning his own electrical firm.

It is also known that he despised Bucky, and maybe because of those feelings he and Lillian drifted apart. Her in Ohio, supporting and defending her husband while he was moving on, electing to move far away and leaving what he would later describe as insanity, behind.

Although they did occasionally speak on the phone and exchange letters through the years, they rarely saw each other while she and Buck were married.

As those years past by, Hank was rarely shy when it came to his opinions of Buck, or his opinions about his own father (which were less than glowing.) His foster care as a child was something he preferred not to discuss or remember fondly as well. And when he spoke of his mother it was often with pity and sadness, and if pressed for reasons his father was absent during those years he would offer little more than a polite, *"I don't know."* Suggesting a few times that he (his father) was a *"ladies man."*

But not much is discussed about Lillian's relationship, or sometimes lack of one with her brother in her diary. Most of it centers around her challenges as a young woman and the family she married into.

And as it nears its end there are hints that Buck and the others won't always be in her life.

Bobby, Patty and Ricky at Lincoln Park School

"I started dating Jim Perkins in 1955. Patty had just started kindergarten at Lincoln Park School and Bobby was in the first grade. I felt that I had to get out. I was so lonely and hating my life. I knew that most of it had been like a living nightmare and I was missing the good old days when I was young and happy.

I was missing my life back home, my childhood, when there were people who loved me and cared about me. I had a great childhood, I really did. But now it was not so great, and I was determined to meet new people and try to start living again. I knew Bucky wasn't coming back, or that if he did nothing would ever change, and Jim was a very nice man.

He was also very handsome and very good to me, and he wanted me to get a divorce and marry him but I just wasn't ready to get married again.

I didn't think I would ever want to do that.

Was it a fear of being married or was there something about Buck that she knew she was not willing to admit? She still loved him, as twisted and completely irrational as that sounds. But was she finally beginning to believe in herself? That she could make it on her own without the challenges she had known previously with marriage?

Or wasn't Jim Perkins convincing enough?

She liked him a lot but she would explain later in life that he wasn't as enthusiastic about her three kids as he was of her. She was a package deal and not only did three kids come with it so did the prospect of a ton of problems from an ex-husband if she were to get divorced and remarry.

Buck doesn't sound like the kind of man who would give up easily. He actually sounds like a guy who could never give up, he was an egomaniac. Maybe *"God's gift to women"* but he was either a curse, or an instrument to test Lillian's faith. A fellow would have to know all of the parables and accept what might come down the road. He would have to be a very good man.

He would have to be the best man Lillian would ever meet.

Willard 1956

Chapter Four

" *I* N JUNE, *1956 I met Willard. I knew it was time to forget Bucky and I knew that I wanted to spend the rest of my life with this man. We began dating and thirteen months later I got that divorce, he was the kindest, gentlest man I ever knew.*

He immediately took to the kids and treated them as his own. He was so good to them, including them in many of our activities together, buying them toys and clothes and even buying Ricky his first tricycle. He was a true family man. Down to earth and liked by everyone around him.

He had served in the Army during the war where he was stationed in France and in North Africa, and when he came home from it he had saved his money while in the service and bought several acres of land in Chillicothe where he and his brothers built a house for his parents.

And like Bucky's family, Willard's folks were country people. But unlike the bunch down in Athens, these were good, hardworking people with higher moral standards. Poor but very decent people.

He was living in a rooming house at the corner of South High Street and Barthman at the time, and he was working in a packing house on Refugee Road called Swifts Premium Meats. But on weekends he would pick me and the kids up and take us to visit his folks, or sometimes we would go to a drive-in movie, or on picnics, and we were quickly becoming like a family.

He was aware of my life with Bucky but he assured me that he would never again be a problem to any of us. I knew he was telling me the truth.

Where Bucky considered himself God's gift to women and thought of himself as "Mr. Romance" Willard was the opposite. A little shy with his emotions and not overly affectionate, (something I missed) but he was everything else I ever thought a man should be.

He was a tall, muscular man and very good-looking, and although he came from the simple world of being a country boy he was very smart and extremely talented with all things mechanical. He liked to work on things and could fix anything. He was also the most polite man I ever met.

In the summer of that year we went house hunting.

Willard did not want to live in Lincoln Park and neither did I so we found a wooden white framed house in the south end just south of downtown in an area called German Village. On a brick street within walking distance of Siebert Street School where the kids would begin classes in 1959, and just a block from a grocery store and a bus stop (I never learned to drive) and only a few blocks from Shiller Park where the kids could play.

It was perfect.

On July 13, 1958 we were married. We did not have a spectacular ceremony, I didn't need one. We didn't go any further than twenty miles down the road for a honeymoon and it didn't last any longer than over night. But I didn't need anything more than what this man was willing to give, a normal life, in a real home with a close family that he would care for and protect."

The house that Willard bought for his new family wasn't anything special, it had been built around the turn of the century and it needed a lot of work, not to make it livable but to make it better, something that he and his young family could be proud of. His new wife was already proud of it, to her it was already a castle. Even before he picked up that first nail and lifted that first hammer, she saw the house as the most beautiful home in the world.

But Willard, whose first name was actually *Jesse* had already built two other houses, one for his parents out in the country and one for his brother Joe to live next door and watch over them.

He typically approached such projects with the attitude that he could make it better, and he always did. He immediately went to work remodeling that house, ripping off worn and tattered wall paper from room to room, tearing up and replacing old linoleum flooring, removing plaster from walls and ceilings, fixing pipes, electrical issues and painting everything that needed painting.

For the next thirty years that is how he spent his vacations and his weekends off, and making that house as nice as he could became his passion, if not his mission. And through those years it would not only be the centerpiece of Lillian's life, but it would become the dome that covered all of her dreams and kept her surrounded by the love that she always knew she would someday find not only for herself, but for the family she always wanted.

When she married Jesse in 1958 he told her that he would care for her and the kids and would never let any harm come to any of them.

Promises he kept.

And when he was not building or repairing things on the weekends he would take the family to Chillicothe for visits and he would take the boys fishing and hunting. Teaching them things he knew and giving them opportunities to learn not just from him, but how to treat others, work hard with them and play by the rules.

Typical childhood mischief would be tolerated to a point, but bad behavior would not, and disrespecting their mother or for that matter anyone else would never be an option. He could be stern but never abusive, sometimes the tone of his voice and the expression on his face was all that was necessary to make them get it.

Every summer the family vacation consisted of a week in Cleveland where Lillian could visit friends and relatives, and show the family the world she grew up in. And what the kids looked forward to most, a trip to Euclid Beach, that wonderful amusement park that Lillian wrote about in her diary and called her favorite place in the world.

Strange, this contrast between the two husbands in Lillian's life. Two men, approximately the same age and from similar geographical backgrounds, both growing up poor country boys in southern Ohio, neither with much more than an elementary school education and both serving in the armed forces during World War ll.

One doing much of his time AWOL, (*Away Without Out Leave*) and on the run from MP's or sitting in some holding cell, the other serving honorably in France and in North Africa during wartime. One who had a history of taking, the other of giving. And one with a hot temper if anyone questioned him or didn't see things his way, the other with a temper just as explosive if someone tried to bully or hurt someone else.

        Bucky   Willard

Away from the sadness and the dangers of Lincoln Park, away from one and two room housekeeping units from Cleveland to Athens and away from people who abused, took advantage of and in general treated her like personal property, Lillian became the stay at home mom she always wanted to be.

Jesse, who was never without a job wanted it that way. Coming from the old school of thought that it was a husband and father's duty to provide for the home and the family, he wanted his wife where she wanted to be, the person in charge of all of that. She never wanted it any other way.

This allowed her to do normal things like join the PTA, get the kids involved in scouting programs, school activities and little league sports, reconnect with old friends from her own childhood and drawing closer to relatives that had been nearly forgotten, like her brother Hank.

The two of them renewed a relationship that would continue for the rest of their lives, making regular phone calls back and forth, writing letters and finally visiting one another even though separated by thousands of miles.

Lillian was finally able to travel to Arizona and he to Columbus. Both were pleased with each other's eventual circumstances.

For the first three years of building a life together everything was going along better than Lillian could have imagined. No broken promises and no surprises, and in 1961 she and Jesse were expecting a child together. Probably the only time she did not fear giving birth, fear of how it would change things.

Instead, she was ecstatic to be giving Jesse a child of his own DNA. However that joy and happiness would not last, she had a miscarriage and the baby was stillborn in 1961. Both were devastated. Nevertheless, it did not change the relationship; in fact they continued to grow stronger together.

Bucky found out where Lillian and the kids were when he was released from prison from contacts he still had in Lincoln Park, and one day he showed up on Lillian's porch and was met there by Jesse. Not much is known about what the two men talked about, but given Jesse's protective nature over his family it can be assumed that he made it clear that Buck would be better off to stay away. In fact, it would be a few more years before he would try again.

Moreover, why he did is something of a mystery. He never called to check on his kids, never contributed a dime to their care or well-being, and he seemed content to never petition the courts for any visitation privileges. But he did come back a few years later, and he requested permission to stop by once in awhile just to see them.

Jesse again met him at the door and told him he had no objection to him being able to visit outside. But that he was to never speak to Lillian unless she spoke to him first, and that if anything verbally was exchanged it had better be polite, and that under no circumstances would he be trusted to take the kids anywhere until they were old enough to decide and fend for themselves.

It would be several years later before he came back.

In 1964 Lillian became pregnant again, and at age 39 she gave birth to Susie and Jesse became the doting, proud dad of a daughter that he would spoil for the rest of his life. But the three kids he inherited wouldn't be denied anything. All four of Lillian's children were his kids, and none would ever feel any different.

Buck's three just gained a sister.

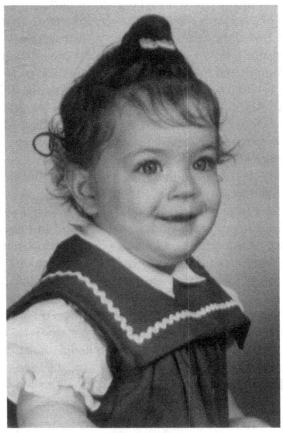

Susie　1964

What these kids would remember most through the rest of their lives was not the man that fathered them, or even much about the unsanitary conditions they lived in before Jesse came along, and not even doing without basic early childhood things. What they would carry with them are the memories of growing up in a safe neighborhood, in a good home and surrounded by other kids to play with, some who would remain lifelong friends.

They would remember living not only in a protected environment, but the love and memories of growing up with a dad that cared for them as well as a mother devoted to keeping them all together, and just as important, what they learned from both of them.

They remained a very close family where being together mattered more than the stories of being with their previous family or of living with strangers. New grandparents, new aunts and uncles and cousins, and none they needed to fear.

And nowhere was that sense of bonding more anticipated or celebrated through the years than during the holidays. Every December 24th was like a chapter from a Dickens classic, or an image from a Courier and Ives collection, with Andy Williams and Perry Como providing the soundtrack filled with holiday classics.

And even in the decades that would pass, when the children were grown and with families of their own, they would all return to the south side of Columbus with new generations to share one of Lillian's greatest passions, Christmas at home.

A bit odd perhaps, for this woman of such strong early Jewish influence to immerse herself so deeply into this particular tradition. There wasn't much written in her diary of Christmases during her childhood, only a few notes about living where presents were opened, but not specific about when. For her to plan for it year round by saving pocket change and trading stamps to buy gifts. And to spend hours each year a few days before Christmas hanging home-made Santa Clauses, paper snowflakes and such.

Or to spend hours tediously decorating the biggest Christmas tree she could fit into her small living room, stringing it with as many bright lights and aluminum ice cycles as it would hold.

And to be so adamant about insisting that the whole family make it home for that holiday and open gifts together, year after year. Maybe that was because she only saw such celebrations in the past from a distance. Or maybe it was because what she once thought would be miracles finally came true.

Rick Minerd

Willard and Ricky 1958

Willard and Susie 1965

Willard and Lillian 1959

Bobby, Ricky and Patty 1959

Willard and Lillian at Euclid Beach in 1961

Ricky and Susie 1965

Patty, Bobby and Susie 1965

Chapter Five

THE FAMILY WAS moving forward, and Lillian was doing everything possible to put her nightmares behind her. That task grew easier by the day, probably from the day she accepted Willard's proposal to get married.

Bucky also started a new life several years later.

In the mid 1960s he remarried, and would go on to establish a new family of his own. He became the father of four more children, two boys and two girls. He would take them on journeys where they would live for a while in different cities, including Columbus, and eventually settle in a small town not far from Spokane Washington.

From the early to mid 1970s he would occasionally try to make contact with his children from his marriage to Lillian but that did not always work out for him. The oldest, Bobby refused to have any contact with him, a grudge he would hold against him forever.

Patty would maintain a relationship with him, but from a cautious distance. Not willing to erase him completely from her life but never trusting him or believing much of what he had say, and not overly eager to see him. Willing, but not necessarily enthused, and usually shaking her head as if humored and in disbelief at the same time.

She is married and has two grown sons Gary and Danny, as well as several grand children.

She and her husband of more than forty years, Mike, reside in Gahanna Ohio.

Bob has a son named Robby, and he and his wife Donna, a retired school teacher have taken up permanent residency in Mesa, Arizona.

Our *little sister* Susie found mom's diary and was kind enough to transform it from her handwriting on discolored sheets of paper onto neatly typed pages that I could work from.

(*Yes, I am the Ricky in this story.*)

Susie is a secretary in her church where her husband Ron is an assistant pastor.

They live in southeastern Franklin County (Columbus).

Bob

Patty

Susie

I returned to the south end of Columbus in 1997 and purchased the house that Jesse bought for us in 1958. Fulfilling a promise I made to my mother as she laid ill, knowing that she was dying of ovarian cancer. She was worried that medical bills might force the sale of the house to *total strangers*. I kept my promise to her that I would do everything I could to see that it never was.

It was her castle, and so far it is still in her family. And we still gather in it during the holidays and keep her tradition going.

My wife Mary and I now live in it and we have five grown children, Ricky, Joe, Kevin, Todd and Kelly, as well as numerous grandchildren scattered about, and in 2005 I retired from law enforcement with the rank of Police Chief.

Irony perhaps.

My mother Lillian passed away in March, 1997 and my dad Jesse followed in August, 1998.

The last decade and a half of his life was spent in constant suffering from the effects of Parkinson's disease and mom's last fifteen were spent as his caretaker. She worshipped the ground he walked on.

My father Buck outlived them both. He passed away in November, 2001 of heart disease. The obituary sent to us by one of his daughters from Washington came with an invitation to *"Everyone whose life he touched, to join in the celebration of a great man."*

The piece called him a *highly* decorated war hero, whose nickname was *"Lucky"* the note stated that he earned that moniker as a boxing champion while in the navy.

Descriptions of a man none of us knew.

Clearly, in his second go-around as a husband and a father he left good impressions.

When I last spoke to him on the phone in the weeks preceding his death he knew that he was dying, and he defended his actions while married to my mother, insisting that *if* he made *any* mistakes it was not his fault. He told me that aside from what it might have seemed, he always loved *us kids* and that Jesse had denied him the opportunity to prove it.

A sweet talker to the end.

The final page of mom's diary appears to be hastily written, as if she were trying to capsulate her life after Buck. Notes with asterisks beside them suggesting that had she felt better, or had more time to complete it she would have written in more detail of everyone she ever knew, especially those who had profound effects on all of our lives.

Notes about relatives on Jesse's side of the family, such as his mother and sister, both who would eventually live with us until they died, and of total strangers who would be taken into our home and helped until they could stand on their own. Some of them children of men Jesse worked with who had been thrown out of their own homes for one reason or another, or childhood friends of ours in similar situations.

It seemed at times that someone was always at the door needing a place to stay, and mom had made notes about Jesse's inability to turn anyone away. At either the door for shelter, or with a broken car that needed fixed or a hand out because they were broke.

The last paragraph in her diary reads-

"My wonderful husband Willard went to work every day, in rainstorms, snow storms, and even when he was deathly sick with the flu, or with pneumonia-just to give our family a good home, and to care for our every need. We never wanted for anything; he was there for everyone, even total strangers. Always finding the good in everyone, he was like a man on call twenty four hours every day whenever someone needed help."

I could not begin to fill in the blanks that she apparently had planned to, and had she been able to finish it herself, I don't know what the title of it would have been. I subtitled it *"A story of Love"* because that is what it is. It is also a road map of sorts, to show others who may be going through what she did, anyone suffering at the hands of someone else, either through abuse or neglect, that there is always hope. That not every bad situation has to end horribly, that it is never too soon to walk away from one.

Lillian began her life in Cleveland with people, who for reasons never fully explained found it okay to move her about from one family to another. And although those early experiences sound like puzzles with pieces missing, she often spoke of being surrounded by love.

Even by the strict disciplinarians who assumed the responsibilities for her early care who did what they could, but to some of us now didn't do everything right. She seemed to love everyone back then and she was still that way at the end of her life.

And by the way, it did end in Columbus, just a few miles from that Greyhound Bus terminal where she wrote about those long layovers years before on those bus trips back to Cleveland, all those times she was running away from Athens just trying to go home.

Not knowing at the time that one day her real home was within walking distance of that terminal, less than two miles actually. Had she focused her gazes from there to the southeast she might have seen the treetops shading the area that would one day become the home she longed for.

And in the days before she passed away she was still speaking in glowing reviews of her family and friends back in Cleveland, and still forgiving Bucky for all that he put her through.

As completely mind bending for me as it is, she did love him. Even though I am sure she knew those emotions were completely wasted on him. Nevertheless, she had them.

Even on her death-bed a month or so before she passed away when he called her after receiving word of her poor health. When she was told that it was him calling she smiled, took the phone and stated, *"Hi Junior, I'm fine, are you okay?"*

It was unbelievable.

First, that she would still be willing to speak to him at all, but then and even more mysterious, why she *cared* how he was doing, but she did.

When they hung up she was still smiling, and all she said about the conversation was *"That man never changes, he is still full of shit."* This from the lips of a woman who throughout her life was offended by curse words, and on those rare occasions when she was mad enough to be tempted to say them, she spelled them.

Her feelings of love for some of the people in her life who didn't deserve them remains a mystery. But her feelings for Jesse and how he changed her life forever is not. That part of her life is unquestionably a love story. All she ever needed to make it so was the right leading man.

All that her kids ever needed was the same thing.

Reflections

I DON'T REMEMBER MUCH about my biological father from the days when I should have known him as a dad, he was not around much, and even if he had been I was only four years old when it became too late for him to come back.

In 1956 I was getting to know my new dad, the man my mother always called Willard and who I called Jesse. I don't know how I know this, but I know he preferred it that way. Not that we both didn't know our respective roles, he was my dad and I was his son, and through my entire life I always referred to him as my dad whenever I spoke of him to anyone, including later in life when talking to old Buck.

That always got his attention. He would snarl and step toward me and say…*"I am your dad!"*

I knew that my reference to Jesse and how I thought of him bothered him but I didn't care. I would welcome that discussion, and I would point out to him that Jesse raised me, taught me how to tie my shoes, ride a bike, bait a fishing hook, get a job, drive a car and he paid the bills that kept me fed, housed, healthy and educated, moreover, with no contribution from him.

I was of course polite about it, never judging him or saying it tauntingly, but crafting the words in such a way as to bait him for certain explanations. His response was generally a rolling of the eyes, and some sort of comment about me not knowing the whole story. However, the invitation to debate his version of it was always available to him. I never suggested that I wasn't open for discussion on the subject.

His forfeiture of an opportunity to polish the image he left behind for all of us to remember was just another olive branch extended to him that he ignored, like all of those presented to him years before.

My memories of Jesse are all fond ones. Of growing up with a dad who spent lots of time with me, always being there, always friendly to everyone, forever playful with my mother and he was a guy I was proud of and hoped to become just like.

To this very day I think I try to immolate who he was. Whenever I'm in a bind or trying to figuring something out I am reminded of those bracelets with the letters WWJD (*What Would Jesus Do?*) I think of that "J" and ask myself, *"What would Jesse do?"* He always seemed to have the right answers, so I'm sure God understands that.

My own spiritual leanings are more mysterious to me than were my mothers, because like her I don't belong to any particular faith but I do believe in God.

Growing up my friends often remarked how lucky I was, and how they sometimes wished they had a dad like mine. Some of their mothers used to tell me that mom was lucky to have such a good-looking, big, strong husband like him.

Once, when I was about ten or eleven I told mom that a friend's mother said she would gladly trade her husband for hers, she laughed and said... *"Tell her she can't have him."*

Because of Jesse she was able to smile often. He made her laugh and seemed to make everyone around him a little happier. Opinionated at times and quick with a corny one-liner, maybe a little sarcasm here and there, but rarely spoken in a hurtful manner. I think it was just his way to solicit a smile, or to make one laugh.

The fact that he only went to school through the seventh grade was merely a statistic. He was one of the smartest men I ever knew, and he was my dad.

Buck on the other hand was my father, and when I speak of my memories of the two men only a few remain that concern him and my early years.

I remember that as a small child I was afraid of him. I recall seeing his temper a few times, and one particular memory of early childhood is vague, but it involves being in the back seat of an old car that he owned. It had broken down on some dirt road in the country.

My sister Patty and I were in the back seat and he told us to stay put as he got out to try to start it. It began rolling backward and we were on an incline, and had it not been stopped by hitting a tree it would have gone over an embankment. I remember being scared and him being mad, as if it were somehow our fault.

That is all I remember about that day.

I also recall going to see him in prison when I was about three or four years old, and mom telling me that we were going to visit him at his army base. I remember the dining hall at the prison and all of the inmates wearing blue denim shirts.

We were having Easter dinner and surrounded by other inmates and other men wearing uniforms. (Guards) Also there that day was his mother (my grandmother) and some of my aunts and uncles.

I remember there was something about all of them that either scared me, or confused me. They were loud people who seemed to cuss a lot, none of them seemed upset about anything yet they were swearing. I also recall asking my father why his uniform was not like the guys with shiny buttons and badges. He told me they were army sergeants and that he was just a private, and that seemed to amuse everyone at the table. I never saw him much after that, or if I did I don't remember much about it.

That is until I was in my teens.

By then he would come by our house once in awhile and ask me to go to Athens with him. He seemed to be quieter, even a little apprehensive when he did, and although he still seemed a little stern, he did have a sense of humor. He would make jokes about how good looking he was, and how women often threw themselves at him, and how he was not afraid of anything or anyone.

He was a very cocky man, small in stature but with a bigger man's confidence in himself.

It seemed important to him to remind me several times that he had given up drinking years ago, not that it mattered one way or another to me, but I believed him. And he seemed happy that he and I were spending time together, always calling me Ricky, or "Son."

On trips with him to Athens to see the others in the family I was more nervous about his driving than I was about seeing people who were mostly strangers to me. (He liked to drive fast) and whenever in the company of my grandmother she would always try to pick my brain about Jesse. She didn't like him at all, and would say that it was his fault that things did not work out between Buck and my mother. She would say something like… *"I hope you don't turn out like him!"* (Jesse)

It is my sincerest hope that, that particular wish is never granted. The highest compliment anyone can pay me is to say that I am just like my dad. Mom said that to me a few times when she pretended to be mad at me or frustrated with me, and she wasn't talking about Jesse. It was her way of telling me I was too full of myself.

If I were to offer personal opinions about myself such as saying I thought of myself as handsome or if I talked about how tough I thought I was, or that I thought girls were lucky to know me, she would say… *"Okay Bucky Junior."*

I never took that as a compliment, and it was never meant to be one.

Still I never hated him, I am not really sure what I felt. I do know that unlike my brother, I am interested in knowing as much about him as I can learn. Bob doesn't even want to hear his name, he has often said that was because he is older than me and remembers more about him.

That's probably true, but even if my memories were as vivid as his I would still want to know as much as possible about my own heritage, and how this man was able to control my mother, and what it was that made life so difficult for him.

Maybe because it never was for me.

My mother went through hell with this guy and there are still mysteries that may never be understood, but I share a bloodline with him and those other rowdy characters talked about in mom's diary, yet I know of no similarities between them and me.

I hope there aren't many if any.

And because of this I never shied away from him, I never wanted to be too close or seem too forgiving of what I knew about him, but I always cracked the door open a little bit in case he wanted to share his side of the arguments.

Like I said before, he never seized the opportunity.

When I was in my early twenties and struggling to become a successful radio announcer and picking up odd jobs to supplement my income I went to work for him. He was a house painter and he gave me a job as a helper for a few weeks, and during that time he never brought up anything about the past.

And if I tried to he would brush it off and prefer to talk about painting techniques. It was all business, sort of like working with a guy you only know. Even when I tried then to bait him for meaningful conversation about his own youth, or his different experiences in life he didn't seem to have anything to share.

Not long after that he and his new family would hit the road and live in other cities and I would rarely ever see him again.

It didn't matter.

In 1989 I was a Franklin County Deputy Sheriff and was responsible for the media relations office. I was good at what I was doing and that caught the attention of someone at the Ohio Police Officer Training Academy (OPOTA) in London, Ohio. They contacted my boss (Franklin County Sheriff Earl O. Smith) and requested that I come to the academy to teach a class on police media relations, which I did.

While I was there I often found myself gazing across the road from the sprawling police academy campus at the London Correctional facility and thinking that thirty years ago my father was incarcerated there. I even shared that with another instructor who saw the irony I was feeling.

The building looked menacing, built around the turn of that century in a weird Gothic looking design with high, thick limestone walls and tall guard towers. Dark gray in color with high barbed wire fencing around it, and I was thinking that I was actually in that place as a little boy to visit my father on an Easter Sunday.

I needed to go there, not on any kind of business, but almost like I was being drawn back to something very mysterious and extremely personal, a desire to revisit something eerie from my own past, and it was as if I would regret it later if I didn't go.

So I arranged through another academy instructor who had connections over there to satisfy something that even I didn't understand, and one day the two of us went to speak to the warden. I told him why I was there and he arranged a tour for us.

(A walk-through.)

There I was, a thirty something year old man wearing the uniform of a deputy sheriff, walking the corridors of cellblocks where my father had once lived for a few years of his life, a long time ago. As I walked I was wondering if I might have passed his cell, if there was still anyone locked up there who might have known him, looking into the faces of old men wondering if I may have seen them there when they were young men.

When I got to the cafeteria, or "mess hall" where we visited Buck and ate Easter dinner all those years ago, I looked at the rows of steel dining tables with attached benches and at the layers on top layers of gray paint that were on them.

I wasn't thinking so much about the overall crudeness of them, or the concrete floor they sat on, or even the foul smell of the area, instead another memory was triggered and I was trying to gather thoughts of my first visit there, and an incident that involved a purple egg.

All those years ago, when as a child I was sitting at one of those tables in that noisy place, having dinner, and I picked up this egg, sniffed it and then threw it on the floor. People were yelling at me and I was trying to make them understand that it smelled bad and it scared me.

Odd even to me, that at that instant I was remembering something as insignificant as a smelly pickled egg. There was so much going through my mind at that moment. I was trying to visualize my mother, hoping I could imagine what she looked like that day, what she wore and what she was feeling.

I couldn't.

But I did know that she was very pretty then, still in her twenties and surrounded by convicts and prison guards, and maybe a target for wolf whistles or remarks that made her feel uneasy, maybe something that would have caused Buck to want to fight someone. He was a very possessive and jealous man.

I could imagine that she might have been a little embarrassed to even be in that place, with people knowing she was the wife of a convict. I was thinking about the environment of our jail back in Franklin County, and the kind of men in there and how I would never want my sweet mother exposed to any of them, or to the pungent smell in there, a smell not at all unlike where I was at that moment.

Jails have an aroma that belongs to only them.

Later, when it came time to leave I shook the wardens hand, thanked him for his generosity and walked freely out of there, thinking I was dressed in something that old Buck probably despised once upon a time, maybe I represented something he feared, the kind of man he tried to avoid, probably often. Then it struck me, I was leaving to go home, something that I am sure he wished he could have done on that particular Easter day back in the middle 1950s when he watched all of us walk away.

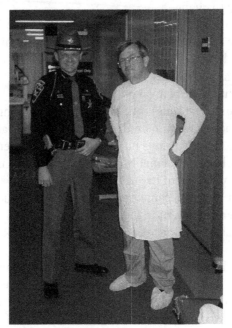

Myself (left) in 1989

However, I can say this about my father; he was not the same man at the end of his life that he was when he was married to my mother. He did eventually turn over that new leaf and become someone else's dad. And I never heard any hint that he was abusive to his second wife, and I know that she adored him.

He eventually got things together and even started his own company, painting and remodeling houses, and the two half-brothers and two half-sisters I have now grew up around a better man than I would have. I also know that had I not gotten a new dad, I would never have become a lawman. As my mother would say, there is no way in H-E-L-L.

I wouldn't have had the proper role model to pursue such an adventure.

But as completely off the charts as this might sound, I think I understand Buck and the kind of man he was. And if I were to write a book about him I think I could impart scenarios of a life wasted on immediate gratifications. A man who couldn't see beyond his own ego, and one who believed his own rhetoric about keeping promises and the ability to change.

I believe he was someone who believed that he somehow deserved to be excused for bad behavior because of his looks, a guy who believed he should have gotten more than he deserved, and none of what he did.

He was right about being a good-looking guy.

Meaner than hell at times, but he did have that going for him, and that one gift mom gave him credit for, that of sweet talk. And when that didn't get him the things he wanted he took it personally.

During my law enforcement career I encountered many Bucky's. I never met any that went to jail thinking they deserved to be there, nor did I meet any who came out rehabilitated or much better than they were when they went in.

It took Buck several years to do that, but I think I understand that too.

For him to let go of his miserable past with my mother it took a guy like Jesse, and he didn't come around until several years after Buck and my mother met. If he had Buck would have been forced to let go and try something different several years before he did. He needed someone to make him understand that it was over, and in that regard Jesse did even him a favor.

Take away the nourishment and the shelter of a rat and it moves on. And in his younger life my father really was something of a rat. But I don't think he was like that at the end.

Although I think I understand some of what he was, and maybe some of the reasons, I remain a little curious about a notation in his obituary. The one that talked about a great man, who was a decorated veteran of World War Two, and why everyone whose life he touched might want to go to the state of Washington to celebrate all he was after he passed away.

The *"Lucky"* moniker is also something of a puzzle piece, although I do remember seeing it tattooed on his arm. But a man who was able to look a better life than he had in the face, throw a punch and then run away wasn't lucky. And for the record his name isn't Bucky, I have chosen to at least protect that.

I declined that invitation as did my brother Bob and my sister Patty, even though he touched all of our lives. If mom were alive then I am sure she too would have declined. She may have smiled, and even shed a tear, because that's how she was. However, I don't think she would have wanted to celebrate how he touched her life.

This postscript to her story isn't meant to put him down or tarnish the memories others may have of him, it is merely a collection of personal thoughts about a guy who happened to be my father, and who didn't seem to get it. Blinded, either by his own arrogance or the belief that he was more than he really was. Maybe he really didn't have anything else to prop him up besides those good looks and the ability to sweet talk his way in and out of things.

Perhaps he was right when he said none of his failures as a husband or a father were his fault, maybe he simply couldn't do it.

I have arrested many men like that.

That regardless of how many second chances some of them get, or how many people try to help them get their lives together, they just aren't able to comprehend. They continue to bite the hands that feed them, then shift the blame onto someone else and make excuses for everything they do.

Thieves can't seem to stop stealing, sex offenders can't stop offending and habitual liars can never tell the truth. But what they can always do is put their problems on someone besides themselves. And what they all seem to expect is for everyone else to excuse them, because many of them also have the gift of conning their way into and out of things. That works more often than it should, and it often accomplishes what it is meant to.

It did with my mother for about eleven years or so.

And when it comes to victims of domestic or social abuse, these people look for and take advantage of weaknesses, or soft hearts like my mother's. Like sizing up their prey and striking out when it suits them, caring only about themselves. Taking advantage of people like her, easy to manipulate and who only have a desire to love and be loved.

He recognized that as soon as he met her. Remember, he asked her to be his wife within days of meeting her. He was like a predator in that regard, and because of what he put her through I could never forgive or excuse him, even though I think I get it.

Not that I think it would have mattered to him either way.

After all, in my last conversation with him he was still in denial, expressing no remorse, taking no ownership of what went wrong, and he was still trying to sweet talk his way around everything, and I know that he expected me to buy it. I think he hung up the phone convinced that I did.

Nevertheless, to paraphrase what my mother said about her last conversation with him, and then to paraphrase something he often said to her, I am good at recognizing bullshit when I hear it. I promise.

For my Mother Lillian, and my Dad, Jesse,
And
For everyone they cared about.

Police Chief Rick Minerd 1958

Printed in the United States
by Baker & Taylor Publisher Services